THE GIRL
With Unshed Tears
& Other Stories

THE GIRL
With Unshed Tears & Other Stories

Suryabala

Edited by
Abhilash Lal

Ocean Books Pvt. Ltd.

ISO 9001:2008 Publishers

Published by
Ocean Books (P) Ltd.
4/19 Asaf Ali Road,
New Delhi-110 002 (INDIA)
e-mail: info@oceanbooks.in

ISBN 978-81-8430-321-6
THE GIRL WITH UNSHED TEARS
& Other Stories
by Suryabala

Edited by
Abhilash Lal

Edition
First, 2015

Price
Rs. 250.00 (Rupees Two Hundred Fifty only)

Printed at
R-Tech Offset Printers, Delhi

PREFACE

Dr. Suryabala is a highly established and widely acclaimed writer, endowed with creative talent, sensitivity and vision. She has contributed substantially to the short story, novel, satire as well as poetry forms of Hindi literature and the canvas of her writing encompasses villages, towns, metros and even foreign lands. She exhibits the open mindedness required in a writer and rises above the narrow considerations of any particular ideology, class or literary movement. Her creative genius thrives on newer milieu and themes with changing backgrounds and, consequently, enables her break new ground in her stories and novels to bare the ever existent human afflictions and anguish.

She does not believe in worn out values but advocates those which are helpful in maintaining our faith in life – and supports the choice to continue in face of seemingly insurmountable odds. Positive contemplation is deeply rooted in her along with a tremendous capability to dive deep into the human psyche and explore their inner thoughts. The merit and the prolificacy of her writing have been recognized through the numerous honours and awards conferred upon her.

The current stories translated into English have not been selected with any plan and cannot be considered representative as they show only a few glimpses of her writing. Some committed readers, captivated by the stories, were moved enough to translate them into English which were published in a few reputed English journals. The translated stories received wide appreciation from the English readers and sowed the idea of bringing out a collection of these stories in book form.

These stories take their inspiration from our inner emotions which are far more profound, vigorous, comprehensive and genuine than the expressed ones. The anguish of deteriorating cultural and moral values pierces Suryabala to her very heart and is the main source of her creativity. The first story of this collection 'House Warming' displays the subtle warp and weft of human relationships which leads to extreme levels of insecurity and dread but, even in such distress, shows the way to a meaningful life.

Another story, 'Homeless', depicts the heights of selfishness and ingratitude as two sons separate their mother and father for their own convenience. Stories like 'Perhaps' and 'The Frock with Yellow Flowers' are based on adolescent feelings and make us appreciate the tenderness that makes our later lives richer and more meaningful.

Suryabala is not a feminist *per se* but fully appreciates and depicts the glory of women with their dignity, integrity and sensibility. Her female protagonists, rather than remain burdened with aggression, complaints and grievances, celebrate their womanhood with a positive approach to the struggles of life and seek their own space. Stories like 'The Final Offering' and "A Woman's Feats' portray an authentic picture of the female character. In the 'Magic Spell', one witnesses an implicit, yet gripping rivalry between mother and daughter while 'Crossing' portrays the intangible and impulsive musings between husband

and wife as the story minutely uncovers the mysterious and touching psychological framework of matrimonial relations. 'Grandpa and Monkeys' touches upon the tragic dimensions of modern society in the loving but ignored grandfather. Facing neglect even from his grand-children, he develops an intimacy with a troop of monkeys – an unlikely bond between a staid and lonely man and the frenzied and rebellious monkeys.

Suryabala's craft and style of writing, enriched with lyrical language, is ever fresh and draws readers with its own magnetism. I am confident that this collection of short stories will by hugely appreciated by English readers.

—Ramji Tiwari

The Story Behind These Stories

On a quiet morning, about 15 years ago, our neighbor walked in with his brother who was visiting. The brother came to know that I was a writer and requested for some of my books to read. I dismissed the request as mere courtesy – how could somebody with Hindi as a third language, ever appreciate the subtleties of characters, situations, idioms and slang which writing relies on?

As a polite brush off, I tried to give him some 'light' reading but finally gave in to his insistence and lent him a couple of my books – having prominently marked the relatively 'simpler' stories.

Completely out of the blue, he called back a few days later.

Contrary to my expectations, he transfixed me with an in-depth and impassioned discussion on all the stories. To cut the story short, not only had he read all the stories, but he had liked them so much that he wanted to share them with all his friends – which would necessitate translating some of them into English given his readers limitations with Hindi.

Not satisfied with my ritual thanks, he was back – to take more stories which he devoured with great pleasure and continued translating them for his friends. Not being a professional translator, he did so merely for his satisfaction, just trying to express the emotions and joy the stories generated in him. And it was his commitment that got me serious about actually getting my stories translated, so they could reach a wider swathe of readers.

Dr. Satchidanandan was most supportive, and that is how the first story translated by this committed reader, Prasad Ghate, was published in 'Indian Literature' as the English story 'Perhaps' (Hindi: '*Kya Maloom*'). This was followed by the English magazines 'Hindi' (published from Wardha under the able editorship of Ms. Mamta Kalia) and 'Pratibha' (run by the eminent writer/editor Sri Seetesh Alok) which published the 'Yellow Flowered Frock' (Hindi: '*Peele Phoolon Wali Frock*') and 'Crossing' (Hindi: *Crossing*) respectively. Additionally, Seetesh ji and the eminent critic, Dr. Ramji Tiwari, also provided their valuable inputs in the translations.

I then realized that Bhisham (Sahni) ji, during his stint with the Sahitya Academy, had commissioned Shree Vinay Jha to do a translation of my story 'House Warming' (Hindi: '*Gruha Pravesh*') for the Sahitya Academy magazine 'Uttara' and the 'Eves Weekly' had published a translation of Hindi: 'Nirvasit' by Mukta Hegde as 'Homeless'. Pooja Birla had also translated a number of my satires including 'Feats of a Woman' (Hindi: '*Ek Stree Ke Karname*'), and Shyam Mathur of Vanasthali Vidyapeeth had translated '*Tilism*' to English as 'Magic Spell'. All these should be enough to make up a collection in book form.

In all honesty, therefore, this collection is not the result of any dedicated effort or plan but it is due to the efforts of all these disparate 'team' members and well-wishers. I have always maintained that just as God himself has no existence without devotees, a writer cannot exist without his readers. All through my 35 years of writing, I have relied on my readers, even more than my critics, for honest and unbiased feedback –

free from embellishments and blandishments – and have been fortunate that my readers have more than repaid my trust in them. Not only have I had the luxury of committed readers but am also fortunate to have had readers who have contributed as translators – an obligation I can never forget.

Dr. Ramji Tiwari kindly consented to write the Preface. And how can I forget the support and contribution of my family, which includes critiques, suggestions, illustrations – and tolerance.

So, dear reader, once again, submitted for your views and kind feedback....

—Suryabala

For Prasad

without whose enthusiastic initiative
this would not have been possible

CONTENTS

1

The House Warming

Biru's letter has arrived, inviting us for the house warming. Filled with ire and love, with taunts and reproaches, invoking a thousand promises dating back to childhood; adding, finally, that 'It would be a real shame if Kunni-Munni (my daughters) do not even know what their *Mama** looks like; if bringing up the name of their *Bua*† registers only blank surprise on the faces of Raja and Bantu (his children). So, if not for your sake or my sake come at least for the sake of these children so that their *Bua* does not remain just the subject of stories for them. So I have fixed an auspicious date and am giving you fifteen days' notice to ensure that *Jijaji*‡ cannot repeat that stale 'can't get leave', excuse once again. Really, I cannot believe that you...... you are the same Didi who..... forget it....

"I almost rush to take Biru's hand in mine and say – why forget it Biru? why have you stopped? Say that I am the same Didi who would carry you on her back all over the place; who bounced you like a ball on a mountain of quilts, and wrung and boxed your ears

---

* *Mama*—Maternal Uncle
† *Bua* —Father's Sister
‡ *Jijaji* —Sister's Husband

when you disobeyed, and because you had dragged my *chunni* in the dust, or clutched my pigtail ribbons to make me a trotting mare and wiped your nose on my frock, right in the middle of a game.

You were thoroughly worthless, extremely naughty, joyously riotous; but still my best friend.

Choked with emotion all day, clutching the letter in moist palms, I wandered around the house doing my daily chores, peeling vegetables, folding the clothes, telling my daughters stories about their Biru *Mama*, Shakun *Mami** and their children Raja and Bantu.

As a little boy, *Mama* used to fly multi-coloured kites with long tails. He would hide under the parapet and cut the soaring kites by throwing little pebbles tied with string across them. Quick as a flash, he would retrieve them and hide them under the sacking in the *barsati.* He would play 'The high-winged *gaajgu*' with the boys and '*Chaak Chaak Chaalen*' with the girls, and have them in splits with his mimicry. Forever ready to visit fairs, shows, marriages, he would keep his few shirts and pants washed, ironed and ready........ he always returned happy from an outing after having thoroughly enjoyed himself playing, eating and making merry. Whenever he was slapped or beaten by mother, barely a couple of tears would have escaped his eyes before he was back in control, and off again after teasing her.

Only once did I see him sad – when a neighbourhood girl was leaving her parents after marriage, wailing and hugging her kin. Standing in the *verandah*, watching, he had asked me then, "Didi, will you also go away like this when you get married?"

"Of course! Do you expect me to stay here all my life?" I had retorted, donning, innocently, the mantle of age and experience. Then in a bid to counter the

---

**Mami*—Maternal Aunt

sorrow of separation that I found enveloping both of us, I continued in the chatty tone of grown-up girls, "But you don't have to worry. I will explain things to your *Jijaji* and come back to see you once in a while."

"OK. Then we will play '*Chaak Chaak Chaalen*' once again," my brother's happiness returned.

"Stupid! By then I'll be a mother. Mothers never play '*Chaak Chaak*...," my mother's full-blooded slap on my cheek broke the sentence—"Shameless girl! Just see the brazenness of this slip of a girl.. Her studies have been brushed aside for the dreams of a 'brother-in-law'. Hadn't I asked both of you sit down to study?..... and here you are, chatting away, disgracefully sermonising about becoming a mother..... you shameless girl!"

I couldn't then comprehend the cause of my mother's anger but I stood shock-still, smarting from the insult of being slapped in front of my younger brother. I don't know what came over my brother then, but he suddenly teased mother, and ran. Mother chased him, desperately, but he ran ahead of her, round and round the *charpoy** lying in the *verandah*, daring her to catch him. He did not stop until the ridiculous sight of my floundering, weary mother and my brother circling the *charpoy* made me laugh uncontrollably despite my tear-lashed cheeks....,

My daughters jumped for joy when they heard about going. "We will go to *Mamu's* house, we will eat milk-and-cream, we will eat ice-cream. OK, if ice-cream costs too much, we will eat little toffees...." and they kept dumping any odd thing they could lay their hands on into my trunk. That hat is for *Mamu's* little one..... what's his name—Raja—it should fit him... and this one-eyed doll we'll give to Bantu. So what if its hair is all in a tangle, we'll wash it with soap....

**Charpoy*—Cot

"Mummy, is there a zoo in *Mama's* town? And what about a children's park? If there is an elephant in the park, we will enter through the trunk and come out from under the tail."

"Shh! Dirty!" The elder daughter mocked the younger.

I washed piles of clothes, ironed them. Repaired the split seams. Segregated clothes for outdoors and indoors and bought cut-pieces to stitch dresses for my brother's children.

On the evening of departure, my husband returned from office in a rush. "We cannot go," he panted, blindly bolting all the doors from inside. "The entire chowk area is full of tension and shops shuttered up right up to *Nai Sarak*. Everyone is in a rush to wind up and is desperately looking for auto-rickshaws to get home. A strange panic is in the air, shops and markets getting deserted in a flash and police patrols moving everywhere, ruthlessly knocking about with their sticks."

"But tell me what happened," I said, more with surprise than shock.

"Much more than what has happened is likely to happen," the panic in his voice had not abated.

"But something must have happened."

"Don't be ridiculous. As if you don't know what happens at times like this; what has been happening—last time, and time and again, every time before that—what can possibly be any different and more frightening than that?"

I tried to assuage his terror and anger, "I only asked because there did not appear to be any tension in this part of the town. Only to confirm whether there is actually some problem or simply the fear of the imminent..."

"Only the fear of the imminent? You think people are crazy? Don't they know what little time it takes for the imminent to turn to reality? They have been through these situations hundreds of times. So, can you blame them if they run blindly, shaking with fear, begging for their lives at the slightest hint of danger?"

"Who is talking of blame? It is quite possible that nothing further may happen or that whatever has happened escalates no further."

"You are sitting in your cosy house, so you can afford to let your imagination and wishful thinking transform things according to your convenience; If only you had also been forced to bolt through the panicstricken crowd – then you would have realised that the fear of dying helpless, struggling to somehow survive, is a more painful experience than death itself." The situation was dragging towards its inevitable resolution.

"Then our going...", my voice drowned in the fathomless depths of despair.

"Are you out of your mind? The entire city is threatening to boil over at any moment and here you are dreaming of going to the station. When you return to your senses, please have some mercy on my condition and make me a cup of tea. Oh...." The children cowered in a corner were listening to our conversation. "We cannot go," I told them and unpacked all the goodies that I had cooked for the journey before them. Bland mouthfuls of food began to melt in their little mouths.

My brother will be there at the station tomorrow. Banking upon his letter invoking a thousand promises dating back to childhood; he will look for us in every single compartment. Even after the entire platform *is* deserted, he will find it difficult to believe that we haven't arrived. *Didi* has let me down once again, he will think. And even out here... tickets, reservation, leave, all had been organised after so much imploring and effort.

The children lost heart, "This is such a horrible town, *Mummy*, isn't it? Such horrible people! Why do they fight so much? *Mama's* town is not so bad, is it *Mummy*? When can we go to *Mama's* town now, *Mummy*?"

And we did arrive, finally. If not for the house warming, at least we did arrive one-and-a-half months later. Loaded, entangled with our trunks, bedding and a tiffin-box. Precisely eight-and-a-half hours late; sweating and exhausted to such an extent that the enthusiasm of meeting everyone had waned. But the children were expectant, alert, showing no sign of sleepiness or tiredness. As the train slowed down sliding into the platforms and I started with delight on spotting my brother standing in the crowd, the two of them shouted out together, *'Mamaji!'*

Pulled by their voices, he came running along with the compartment. The same thin face with the same old flush of joy. Even more excited than the children.

I stroked his head with my hand... as if he were a little child, "You must be really tired and bored, what with the one O'clock afternoon train reaching at nine-thirty in the night."

"At least it has arrived. I had come prepared for nine-thirty tomorrow morning," his face was radiant with happiness. Just then there emerged from the crowd a thick, heavy set, cheap sinister-looking figure mounting a pinch of chewing tobacco crushed on the palm.

"So, you have arrived. Heh heh heh heh!" An utterly uncouth laughter slipped out through the stained teeth. My daughters stared at the apparition on the sly, with a mix of fear and curiosity. I tensed up but my brother intervened hurriedly, trying to pre-empt the daggers-drawn exchange of looks between us.

"Oh Yes! They have arrived. But where had you gone?"

"I spotted a '*paan*' shop and I replenished my stock of lime and tobacco... Heh heh."

"*Jijaji*, this is my friend Bhurelalji from the same locality... and these are my sister and her husband," my brother introduced us.

"That I could make out at first sight, *yaar*... Why do you shower us with these philosophies?"

I was about to lose my temper when a reed-thin boy also appeared. "This is Manoj, our neighbour," said my brother.

My husband and I sat on two separate *rickshaws*, each with one daughter because the luggage wouldn't fit into a single *rickshaw*. My brother and Manoj took their respective bicycles.

"I hope everything is alright. You carry on, I'll settle my stuff in minutes and join you later." Bhurelal winked at my brother on the word, 'stuff' and turned his motorcycle in the opposite direction.

I thought my brother had changed so much; imagine keeping company with such coarse, loutish friends. My face was flushed with anger.

Piercing the dark, clanging their bells, the *rickshaw-pullers* pedalled away, rhythmically springing on their toes. My brother and Manoj covered the front and rear respectively, on their bicycles. Suddenly, Bhurelal's motorbike overtook us and went ahead in the dark.

"Is this man your friend?" I asked.

My brother laughed sheepishly, cycling alongside, "I had figured out from the look on your face at the station itself... It is because of the night – what with children and so much luggage – that I had requested

Bhurelal to come to the station. In any case, it is always better to be friends with a couple of such people in your locality, wherever you are."

"What do you mean by such people?"

"What I mean is," my brother stumbled again. "He is just what he appears to be. You would have realised this from his forbearance. A kind of bad character of the locality we stay in." He bent his head in shame, thinking of my daughter sitting beside me.

I raised my head to look all around—nothing but deep, unfamiliar, unfriendly darkness all around. No sign of streetlights. The place did not look inhabited in the least; only a forest of darkness filled with frightening silence.

"Is everything normal here?" my voice betrayed my fear.

My brother, sensing my fear, replied with an accentuated casualness, "Oh Yes, absolutely fine. There is no problem at all."

"How can you say absolutely fine, *Bhai Sahab*?" Manoj interjected bringing his cycle close. "Why don't you say that people avoid going out alone after nightfall here. Incidents of theft and snatching are commonplace even around the Civil Lines area. Just the day before..."

Before Manoj could say anything further, desperately, my brother cut him, "It is nothing like what you are saying. These things can happen anywhere sometimes. You people get upset very quickly."

After Manoj's incomplete sentence, my eyes constantly followed the tail-light of Bhurelal's motorcycle, frightened and grateful. My mind was in turmoil. The expectation of seeing my brother's halfbuilt house, his children and the happiness of meeting Shakun after ages and sharing her laughter had all evaporated. Here I was, now drifting in a dark ocean of fear, my frightened eyes trying to penetrate the darkness; imagining all the possible terrible things that could happen. All worldly attachments, the excitement, Shakun and the children had vanished in a flash.

"Here we are. This is Biru's palace."

By the time we disentangled ourselves from the loaded *rickshaws*, a gush of excited, cheerful voices sprang from within the house. Then there was Shakun, shaking with happy excitement, hopping towards us, shy yet eager to say as much as possible, as quickly as possible... for a while there was a confusion of voices. The most excited was my brother, straddling four to five wavelengths at a time, "Now will you let them freshen up first, Shakun, instead of welcoming them with your taunts and complaints... Hey Raja, why do you stand there now like a zombie in a corner! And look at the elder one, *Jijaji*, he has become such a roly-poly fatso. And he used to be such a waif when he was small... *Bantu*, won't it be fun now! You have two little sisters to protect you now in the fights with your brother."

Bhurelal entered the house mouthing another pinch of tobacco, "All OK brother Sharma, I can go now."

The voices ceased. My brother gathered his wits in a moment and said, "Oh yes, yes" but Shakun came forward with a glass of water and a plate of sweets saying, "How can you leave like this?..." By then I had opened up the box of sweets I had brought before Bhurelal with a look of deep gratitude. My brother watched me surreptitiously, probably trying to make himself believe the change in my attitude.

"Come *Jijaji*, let me take you around the *Diwan-e-khas* of Biru's palace," my brother's hospitality continued after he had seen off Bhurelal at the door.

"You had entered through the front *verandah*..., now these are two rooms... or," he paused, "You can call them roomlets. These roomlets have been erected but the wall-plastering is yet to be done. If you ask me why, I will tell you that this effort has consumed all the bricks, concrete, lime, mortar and money available.... Therefore, even the boundary wall is reduced to being merely symbolic. The leftover lime and mortar have been collected to beat out the platforms for this kitchen so that arrangements for food are established... Look at it this way—isn't this good enough for a family slightly below the average income index—what do you think, *Jijaji*, eh? From the point of view of location, it is not really outside the town – just on the outskirts...the only problem being that the children's school is a little far off...."

"And the slaughterhouse slightly near..." added Shakun, smiling. My brother ignored his wife's comment and went on, "I'd rather say – what's wrong? It will only give the children some exercise...of course, the continuous thundering from the narrow gauge railway passing beyond the backyard doesn't let up all day and is irritating at night, but I am sure we will get used to it soon. Some people say that houses built near railway lines and bridges weaken very quickly...but we don't have to build a *Qutub Minar* that we need to worry...and the main thing is, *Jijaji*, that if we had gone in for so many calculations, then there would have been no house to live in. If nothing else, we are saving at least ₹ 375 on rent, though, at present, I am repaying four hundred and fifty rupees on account of the house-building loan. But how does this matter, once the loan is repaid after eight to ten years, there will be contentment.

There was childlike enthusiasm on my brother's face, a reflection of a prosperous world many years hence, but I found Shakun smiling. A spectator's smile at the desperate antics of a clown trying to make the audience laugh; a smile laced with pity.

My brother caught on, "Why do you look at her, *Didi*? You listen to me...everything from the flour-mill to the Government hospital is within a walking distance from here."

"The Government hospital...," Shakun couldn't contain herself now, "They all say that it is better to take a patient to the cremation ground; it will at least save *rickshaw* fare."

"And the free-flowing *Gomti* river, close by." My brother continued on his own stream, ignoring Shakun.

"Please ask him, *Didi*, who will trudge a mile and fetch any amount of water? Will he do it himself?"

"Let the opportunity come." My brother continued light-heartedly.

"Of course" my husband also joined the fray. "If nothing else, we can at least camp on the river bank."

My brother turned, a little embarrassed, fearful for a moment that his brother-in-law might be pulling his leg. But he saw only jest in my husband's eyes and returned to his old position, fortified.

"Laugh, if you will, but at least you will never be in danger of dying of thirst."

"And when there is danger of the ground floor flooding and getting washed away, what then? They all say, *Didi* that whenever floods come, there will be no sign of this house built in a ditch..."

OK, OK, let it drown when it has to. This town has seen only drought condition for the last two years, with God's grace. Even my brother laughed this time.

"Please ask him, *Didi*, if it will remain dry here forever."

Now my brother lost his temper.

"Then why don't get yourself allotted a house on a hilltop? Who is stopping you? Or else, an impressive bungalow in the Civil Lines compound. It will cost you only seven *lakhs*, get it? He then turned to us, pleading," "Now you tell me *Didi*, should such things be said...which town in India does not have floods? What? Even big cities have floods. Towns, big and small, get wiped off. Don't the houses of the most affluent in the cities submerge in the floods?"

It seemed Shakun had forced herself into silence, a silence clearly stating, "So, we have at least this one thing in common with the affluent."

"And look at this, *Jijaji*, this large space left vacant at the back. It was only because of an empty purse that I made an apology of a boundary wall. I thought that things will get done when we have money. In any case, the space is being put to its best possible use at present."

We saw that our children were playing, running, jumping completely oblivious of the world around.

My brother was delighted, "Now you tell me, could the children have ever dreamt of such an open space in that foot-wide street and the two matchbox rooms? Could they have had such fun and frolic?"

It seemed Shakun was silent despite having a ready reply. She diverted my brother's attention, "Let's go, now that *Didi, Jijaji* have seen the house. I will lay the table now."

When it came to sleeping arrangements after dinner, a fresh dispute broke out. One of the children spoke of sleeping on the rooftop and the others joined in a happy chorus. Even my brother was happy with their excitement. But Shakun, smiling through a face draining of colour, refused to accept the proposal.

The children sniveled and pleaded for long but Shakun continued to skirt the issue without really giving any concrete reason for her refusal. On the other hand, my brother was bent upon accommodating them at any cost. "You are unnecessarily spoiling the happiness of the children," he blurted out suddenly, irritated.

"Unnecessarily?" Shakun's low voice became barbed, and she stood still, her pointed stare boring through my brother.

He squirmed; so did the children.

Shakun took my brother aside and whispered, "Why do you act so naive before everyone? It has hardly been ten days since across-the-bridge Guptaji's.....," she remembered the children and fell silent.

"Oh, come on! Guptaji's daughter was very young. And these children are older and more sensible.... and just because of an incident or two...."

"I do not want to get into an argument. The children just won't go to sleep on the rooftop. Only ten feet high and a dry, open drain all around. The trains invariably slow down over the bridge...if someone gets away on one of those, even a lifetime's search will be futile."

Suddenly, I shivered from head to toe, a goose pimple shiver that jangled every pore in my being, but I quickly controlled my voice and said, "I do not understand the need for so much argument and counter-argument. Once *Bhabhi** has said no, that's it! No more pleading. The children will sleep right there, on the kitchen *verandah*."

Surprisingly, no one countered this time. My brother was relieved that the end of the argument gave him a chance to come and sit with me, relaxed. Ignoring exhaustion and the oppressive heat, he planted himself by my side.

**Bhabhi*—Brother's wife (sister-in-law)

My husband dozed off the minute he lay down. My brother and I reminisced about our school, the *chilbil* tree, the plum-hill and the topknot of our Sanskrit teacher. Of how my brother had once drawn a mustache on the face of my clay milkmaid...and I had just cried and cried...crying, I had gone to wash her mustache under the tap. When I looked at her afterwards, I found that along with the mustache, her eyes, nose and lips as well had been washed away.

My brother clapped his hands and teased me, "Yes, and when you had thrown away all my rose-apples* in fit of anger, I had gnashed my teeth in a rage and bitten your arm; do you remember?" he laughed, sheepishly.

"Why wouldn't I remember? Look...." I rolled up the sleeve of my blouse to show him three little tooth-marks.

The marks were deep, and he was embarrassed.

"Yes, and that...."

"The rest tomorrow morning......get up now. Let *Didi* sleep and please lock the doors," Shakun interrupted.

Brother got up, unwillingly, and the two of them began securing the doors with two to three bolts and chains. Then came the turn of the locks, with three or four locks being used on the rear doors.

When I asked, Shakun explained, "The boundary wall is hardly anything, *Didi.* The entire house is like a served-out plate. Every evening, I carry all the stuff inside, big and small. Only last week, I had forgotten my husband's vest and trousers outside. By morning, they had vanished...."

"Oh no! I've spread my *saree* out to dry, outside...."

"I brought it in, long ago this is a daily routine...."

And despite eyes drooping with exhaustion, she checked every lock and chain to ensure that they were

*Rose-apples—Berries

properly secured. As I was trying to sleep in the silence of extinguished lights, I heard whispers from the children's *verandah*....

"How big was Guptaji's little girl? As big as *Chhoti*?"

"How old is *Chhoti*? That girl was two years younger than Minu."

"Had you people seen her?" my younger daughter asked, tentatively. "Of course, she would play with us only. She would create a scene if we didn't allow her to play. But she was much younger in any case, so we would keep a substitute for her because, when subsided, she saw the thief coming towards her when playing *catch-catch*, she would run, crying loudly; she was so young, you see. She was frightened even at the mention of the thief but she still wanted to play. I wonder how terrified the real thief would have made her."

"Is that why Gupta *Aunty* cries so much, isn't it?"

"Yes, because they all say that thieves burn or break the limbs of little children and force them to beg." This was my brother's child.

"I had seen in a film, you know, that the thief stole a child. Then asked his *Papa* for a lot of money and instead of returning the child, pushed him down the hill...."

"Minu! I am scared." This was the nervous, pleading voice of my brother's younger son.

"You hide your eyes and mouth under the sheet." My elder daughter appeared to test my brother's elder son, "Are you frightened?"

"Why do thieves come only at night?" The listener seemed to cling to his neighbour asking this question.

"Yes, but do you know that a thief entered the house of an *Aunty* in our colony in the afternoon after ringing the bell. Actually, at that time, there are no *Papas* or children at home, so *Aunty* thought that her children had returned. The thief drew out a knife but that *Aunty* was very brave. She grappled with him and kept shouting. Finally, when a couple of people ran to help, the thief bolted but *Aunty* was quite badly hurt."

"Even in the house of our *Aunty* at number seven, you know, some time ago three-four persons barged inside one evening with pistols and said that if you want the safety of your husband and children handover all the keys immediately.... We overheard the round of pistols being fired in the air...as they threatened."

"Then?"

"Just then their servant returned from the market with vegetables and entered the kitchen through the back door. The moment he realised what was happening, he rushed to the roof and screamed like mad. And the robbers ran away. Otherwise, they would have looted everything and killed Uncle, Aunty and everyone so that they could not be identified later on."

"That's why they cover their faces."

"Hey...stop, all of you."

"*Chhoti* is frightened...."

"And are you not?"

"Let it be; no one will talk about thieves or say frightening things any more."

In the morning, a blanched-white sun hid under the mist, and the dew-moistened breeze waved lazily, intermittently. A morning, like a loving gift, in the hot summer and the spirits soared with freshness. The children never rose so early but today, in the excitement of being at *Mamu's* house and a new place, they were up early and were now going up and down the stairs, scampering all over the house.

The dew-wet grass on the slope near the railway line and the bridge was green and fresh even in the summer heat because of moisture from the *nullah*.

"The weather is really nice...come *Didi*, let us sit there and have tea.... Shakun, you also join us for tea. It would have been fun if *Jijaji* were also awake... after all, you have come only for a week."

As he sipped his tea, brother kept advising Shakun on what to cook for breakfast, lunch and dinner, ordering all kinds of things.

"Make sure that there is an omelette for *Jijaji*. Use the spoon to whip the egg...get it, Shakun? Some toast also, but for *Didi* please make some *kachories*.... Will *porridge* be alright for children or *suji halwa*, Shakun?... *Didi*, Shakun makes delicious stuffed *karelas*.... Please make dinner well in advance...for we will go out in the evening, either to the Gomti, or the park at Civil Lines or else the *Neelkantheshwar*... anywhere...simply going out together is a special thing."

"But well before it is dark," this was Shakun. My brother glared and Shakun fell silent.

Then it was at if brother was talking to himself, "In any case, it gets dark very late in summer. It's alright, we will return early so that there is no problem getting *rickshaws* what with the children's brigade."

In the meanwhile, the children came running, jumping towards us and brother's son Bantu declared innocently, "We will go to the bridge. Barey (Raja) says that it is very near and he will take us all around."

As expected, Shakun screamed from the kitchen the moment she heard him, "No one is going anywhere. We are all going out together in the evening in any case. And don't you people want your breakfast now?"

"Breakfast is not even ready yet," Mantu muttered resentfully. Then he looked at me, controlled himself and announced to the children, "Come on, let's play robbers. I have three pistols."

"Three pistols," I murmured, and Shakun said, "What can I do, *Didi*? I don't know how he has picked up this craze for collecting old toy pistols. He has asked all his classmates and friends to give him their old and useless pistols. Only last week I threw away two that I found while cleaning the cupboard, into the *nullah*. I don't know where he has found these now...."

A loud bang made me jump out of my skin, but Shakun was unperturbed.

"This is Mantu's mischief. He stashes away these Diwali crackers to create these bangs while playing."

I couldn't resist the temptation of looking. Peeping quietly from behind the door, I got the shock of my life. Brother's son Mantu had donned a vest and belt, covered his face with black cloth; like a dangerous dacoit, holding pistols in both hands, talking so harshly that even I shivered. Along with his friends, he was threatening an entire 'family', calling the housewife a 'flashy-woman', threatening to riddle everyone with bullets if his demands were not met. One of the children who had come to play was being kicked around, while two small children cowered in a corner, actually frightened.

"Breakfast.... Breakfast; come on, let us have breakfast first." I said as if to free myself from my own fears.

After breakfast, the games continued. There was a terrible accident involving a car and three scooters and for a long time there was much wailing and shouting on this account. After that the mention of a train brought us some relief. Betel, *bidis*, soda, whipped curd and hot tea were sold on the platform. The train whistled and rolled away and then tumbled down the bridge producing such screams and terrible commotion that we found it difficult to stay around...the children didn't need any rehearsal for screaming. The noise of their playing became so loud that Shakun hurried to scold the children.

"Don't they ever play with dolls?" Brother asked, irritated.

"What generation are you talking about?"

"Perhaps our own time," I laughed beset with memories but brother was already down the memory lane "Yes, I think once every six months at least one or the other doll of yours got married. You had an entire clan of dolls."

"And we would cook *puries* and sweets on a little stove."

"We would collect wild flowers and leaves and prepare the ceremonial canopy. Wrap shining cigarette paper on tiny bamboo sticks."

"Yes, and we had collected a box full of cigarette wrappers together."

"Whole day, we would be busy arranging ornaments, decoration, clothes for the dolls and decorating the ceremonial courtyard."

"All of us boys would blow trumpets and play the drums stuck with red and yellow paper bought from the fair, all day."

My brother looked thoughtful for a moment and then burst out laughing, "The funniest was when you and your friends decked up in six-yard *sarees*, showing off, addressing each other as '*Behanji*' talking of the problems of your dolls as if they were sons and daughters. Everyone would be laughing through clenched teeth."

"But then we never had the time to see who was laughing at us. At the top of our voices, we would be singing wedding songs and dancing.... Oh the bride, my darling, has lost her heart to the groom...."

Suddenly, Biru said, "Do you remember that Radha? She who whirled round and round and waved all over while dancing?"

"Yes, I remember her quite well."

Brother's voice faded as if drowning, as if he couldn't decide whether to tell me or not—"Do you know, she is almost insane now, after the accident involving her husband and both children...?"

"Accident? How?"

"Nothing; just like that. They were returning from the market on a scooter when her husband stopped at a '*paan*' shop as the children were whining for toffees and Radha had asked for *meetha paan*."

Radha was standing by the scooter. Just as he turned after collecting the toffees and paan, five-six bullets sprayed from a passing motorcycle felled him and both the kids. Only Radha was spared...."

The fear shook me physically. A terror-filled shivering gripped me as if Radha's husband and two innocent children were struggling before me, soaked in blood....

"But why? Did they have enemies? Or some rivalry?"

"No such thing.... some people say they were killed, mistaken for someone else. Others say it was done simply to spread terror among people."

My brother stopped since Shakun was returning from the kitchen. Quickly, we changed the subject. "Do you remember Biru, how we would play-act Sheikh Chilli and the clown – 'panda'?"

"And right from class three and four, you would make us play patriotic games. Most of them on Fifteenth August and on Gandhi-Jayanti. Whatever you saw in school, you would make the neighbourhood children perform after you returned home. Poetry, *Antaksharee* and the Flag hoisting. I liked that song the most...."

"Which one? Immortal be the fame of our Flag."

"Yes, Yes...", said my brother with childlike enthusiasm.

Suddenly as I began to hum the tune, as if looking for its source, my brother caught on and handed down the words...we hummed together, then in a moment, both of us began to sing together. I drew the first sentence....

Saffron, cloth in fine silk,
resplendent may this, our land be.

My brother picked up the second line....

Abundant with crops, rich and green,
more beautiful than this constant world may this our land be.

Then our voice got carried away, like two boats, in a torrential flow....

More beautiful than the constant world,
may this our land be.
Respondent may the land be....
Resplendent may our land be....
Resplendent may this land be....

Surprised with ourselves, flowing along the stream of our voices, we went from one verse to the next. It must have been years since the passion and freedom of my brother's voice had burst forth. Accompanied by the thin, wriggling stream of my voice, a spring of notes had gushed out from my brother's throat. Suddenly the spell broke. The children had abandoned their game. *Jijaji* had put aside his detective novel and they were all standing around us, applauding. Shakun, browning onions and spices in hot oil for seasoning the *'dal'*, was smiling.

"I think in their time, this brother-sister team must have collected a good deal of money going around the neighbourhood, singing together" The brother-in-law joked.

But the children stood smiling, looking at us with curiosity and admiration.

And I was thinking, "Shakun looks so beautiful when she is comfortable, relaxed and smiling freely. Why can't she be like this all the time?"

But that was not to be.

Next morning, as I was squeezing toothpaste on to my brush, the open space in the back was the scene of great commotion. I heard my brother's vexed whisper, "Talk softly otherwise *Didi-Jijaji* will wake up."

The moment she saw me, Shakun, animated and breathless, started off, "Look at this *Didi*; clear footprints from the boundary wall upto here. Now you tell me, do these belong to an animal? I say somebody must have scaled the wall last night.... but my husband refuses to understand. He says why would a thief come, only to return empty-handed? Please explain to him that it is possible one of us might have woken up to go to the toilet and the thief must have lost courage on seeing a light switched on. Or it is possible that the thief might have presumed these to be ordinary locks whereas I had used genuine Aligarh locks brought from my Uncle's place. I could bring only these locks, and nothing else, when I went there last year. The house would have been robbed if it were not for these locks...."

There were tears in Shakun's eyes but my brother found it utterly unpalatable, "So what if one had got robbed? Is there some great treasure of the cousin of Moses buried in our house? What? You have a habit of making a fuss...what is the point now in making an issue out of the question whether a thief came or not? And now look; you have woken up *Jijaji* also; are you pleased with yourself now? Will you give them some tea now, or you will continue with your court and interrogation?"

"I have already put the tea to boil," Shakun said softly. "But are *Jijaji* and *Didi* outsiders that we need hide anything from them? Now you tell me Didi, aren't our greatest treasure the children...?"

My brother's glare and Shakun's voluntarily biting of her tongue, leaving the sentence unfinished, happened together in a flash of a moment but the faces of the three children had drained of colour.

Then it seemed as if my brother was manfully jumping into a river to save the lives of many drowning persons, all together, "Come on, let's get some *jalebies* for breakfast today. Shakun, I am declaring a holiday for you. *Jijaji*, there is a little *halwai's* shop at the next crossing. The shop is a little shanty, but he makes his *jalebies* absolutely crisp and tasty.... *Didi*, do you remember that fellow, Nanku *halwai* near our old house? Whenever I went to fetch something from his shop, he would invariably give me four *jalebies*, separately in a leaf-cup, apart from the purchases. But you would never let me enjoy all four *jalebies* by myself. The moment I entered the lane where our house stood, you would appear from behind the door and say, come on, take out Nanku's *jalebies*...."

The children burst out laughing. Slowly the "foot-prints" were erased from everyone's mind.

In the evening, brother brought spiced fried *pakoras*, and for the night yummy '*Rabri*', It was worth watching the staring, peeping, greedy eyes of all the children. In our own homes, neither my children nor my brothers' could have afforded *Rabri* or *cream* in normal course. There would be a greater squeeze whenever guests came, but my brother seemed to be blowing up money in a stupor of exhilaration. Shakun would stop him, "There were sugar crusted dough-lumps and I would have boiled vermicelli in milk; what was the need to throw away twenty-five rupees?"

But brother laughed and sat down after dinner to rally the children and distribute the *Rabri* in proverbial wise-monkey style. Once the earthen pot was empty, he whirled it over his head in the style of a discus – thrower, beyond the bridge and said, "OK, the children's brigade will now take to their heels and go in and play in the *verandah* or tell stories, jokes, or play *'antaksharee'* or whatever comes to their minds...we will spread a sheet in this courtyard and sit over a pack of cards. Is that right, *Jijaji?*" And he looked at us as if he were giving us a big surprise. My husband and I were moved.

The children had never been showered with such affection, had never experienced such ostentation or indulged in so much fun and food in their living memories. For them, Mamu had become an angel from heaven and they would be at his beck and call, fighting each other to get to him first the moment he expressed a wish.

"Shakun, please get the chequered sheet, I have already asked Manoj to join us in the afternoon." He seemed to be congratulating himself on his impeccable and flawless planning.

"Come *Didi*...Shakun, join us once you wind up your kitchen and show *Jijaji* your skill...they think you are innocence personified. Let them also see your deftness." Shakun actually joined us immediately, smiling. So did Manoj.

Quickly, the cards were shuffled, mixed and handed out. Equally speedily did Shakun's quick gestures, sly exchange of information with her partner bring disaster and defeat to the opposition. After all the laughter and frivolity, my brother was now on the verge of losing his temper, frustrated with the continuous defeats. He began to keep a close watch on Shakun to catch her hinting to her partner.

Just then, surprised and nervous, Shakun whispered in a frightened voice, "Listen, it seems somebody has thrown a stone, right next to me...."

"OK, OK, since you didn't get favourable cards this time, you are trying this new ploy."

"Come on, *Yaar*! You should understand moves other than those in a mere game of cards. Even love-letters come wrapped around stones." *Jijaji* jested.

But before he could finish, three or four more stones rained through the dark and fell in the courtyard, one of them right below my shoulder....

Everyone rushed to one side. Agitated, my brother made a move to rush to the boundary wall but my husband and Manoj stopped him. It would have been sheer stupidity in any case because beyond the four-and-a-half-foot boundary wall, it was absolutely dark for a considerable distance. The circle of light was only over our chequered sheet so that those outside could see us, but we were unable to see anything at all beyond this circle... There was nothing else around, no houses, no huts, no shops, no habitation whatsoever.

Our faces were frozen with a different land of fear, misgiving, anxiety, and dejection. There was silence, except for the intermittent rustle of wild bushes or leaves, or the movement of an animal; the rustling made the silence even more frightening. The stones continued periodically. Shakun's blanched face was turning paler by the moment. And my brother, distressed, defeated, seemed to be explaining things to himself with a strangely pitiful expression, "I cannot figure out who these people are. Who can it be, so late in the night, doing a meaningless thing like hurling bricks and stones in the dark?"

"*Didi*....", suddenly Shakun's timid, distinct and drowned voice seemed to float to the surface, "It is all my fault. From the day that I...."

"You just shut up," my brother rushed, almost closing her mouth, "You are always thinking and talking baseless stuff. It is nothing *Didi*. It is just possible that some stupid boys must be passing this way; they have a habit of needlessly flinging pebbles, kicking around when they go anywhere." Though no consolation, my brother's words seemed to reassure us...he was further encouraged, "Look even the stones have stopped now...let's get back to the cards."

Shakun was still unnerved. Not in the least consoled by my brother's words nor in favour of continuing the game outside. But brother was bent upon, carrying on, as if it were a matter of honour. The others were torn between the two of them... seeing no alternative I found a compromise. "Come Shakun, let's go inside and chat while these three settle down to play outside."

Shakun came in quickly, but there was apparently nothing to talk about. I struggled to pick up threads of conversation... "Yes, how is the children's school? Is the teaching alright?"

"Oh!," Shakun would catch on with a start, "Good...but it is very far. A mile, along a lonely stretch of road, *Didi*. These days I drop the children myself."

With feigned naturalness, I kept trying to drag her into conversation about all and sundry. But Shakun, purely out of deference, just kept up the conversation with her brief replies. Suddenly we heard the players outside get up. Their excited whispers filled the air. "Let it be, we will go inside Biru. No, No that side, let us go into that house."

"It is definitely some kind of conspiracy, someone seen to be threatening, or else why should this happen so late night?"

"I hope you haven't made an enemy of someone."

"Or you, Manoj?... Is the liquor vendor trying to grow this land...?"

"What is it?" Shakun got up, hysterical.

"Nothing." My brothers' voice sounded hollow.

"The stones are being hurled again, aren't they?"

Manoj nodded in agreement with Shakun, avoiding my brother's eyes. My husband leaned against the wall and lit a cigarette.

"Now what? What will happen now?" Shakun's lament broke her restraint and burst out. "How can we live here? You will go away after a couple of days *Didi*,... just think of my plight...if something happens to my children...."

"Come on now, Shakun. Why do you keep jabbering like the uneducated and ignorant? Is this some anarchy....?" I felt more pity for my brother than for Shakun. His face belonged to a defeated, hopeless man whose repeated valiant and enthusiastic efforts to set things right had fallen flat, whose every positive move had backfired.

"Of course, this is anarchy. Tell me *Didi*, what can be more unjust than this. I say there is definitely some conspiracy..."

"It is nothing. Brooding, all by yourself, you have nursed these irrational fears deep in your mind," I rebuked Shakun affectionately.

My brother looked at me, gratefully and the defeated warrior got back some of his courage. He returned to the battlefield, "Exactly, this is what I also say... there is nothing to get upset about. I have a feeling that this is a prank by some depraved undesirable elements...come on why don't we play inside the house, *Didi?*"

He looked at me for support, "Oh yes, why not?" I was with him wholeheartedly.

"You want to play, Manoj?"

"Please carry on *Bhaisahab*.... I was about to leave in any case," Manoj replied in an indifferent, weary voice.

"Yes...let it be," my husband lit another cigarette.

My brother was now openly defeated.

"OK.... I will leave now...," Manoj was tense, fearful. My brother understood the request in his statement and said, "Oh? Yes, Yes, I will accompany you outside."

"I'll also come with you," my husband said.

The moment they left, Shakun rushed to my side and sat down as if she would never get another opportunity to do so and blurted out in a whisper.

"*Didi*, please try to convince my husband that he must sell this house and return to the smelly-hole in that narrow street."

I was surprised, "What has happened to you Shakun? Because of a small matter like this, you are planning even to sell this brand new house of your own, built after so much difficulty and with such enthusiasm."

"The house is not more important than the children, *Didi*."

"Now I really lost my temper," "Why do you unnecessarily keep fearing for the lives of children, Shakun? Is it just because of that single episode involving Guptaji's daughter?"

"It is not just that, *Didi*. You don't know the whole story."

"What is it that I don't know? Why don't you tell me then..."

"Right here, on the railwayline slope, hardly a week ago, on a blazing desolate dreary afternoon, with hot wind blowing...," Shakun's whispering voice was getting more excited and hurried.

"But what happened?"

"The children were indoors after their lunch. Oppressed with afternoon heat, I was trying to wind up the kitchen when I heard something falling again and again. Then came a suppressed, suffocated infant scream.... I felt a strange sensation, *Didi*, I left the kitchen and by the time I had reached the boundary wall, my hands and feet went numb. On the railway-line slope, a man kept lifting up a child, and each time the child struggled to release himself from the man's grip, in a rage he would fling the child to the ground hard...till finally the child lay motionless, exhausted. Then the man caught the child by the neck under the chin, stung him over his shoulder like a cask and tried to rush up the slope. The child's eyes were popping out, bloodshot, insect like, the limbs were flailing but its voice had choked."

Shakun was breathless, so was I.

"Then?" My own breathing was fast, laboured.

"I began to scream at the top of my voice as if I had lost my mind, and hurled bricks, stones whatever came to my hand scattered near the parapet towards the slope."

I cannot even remember things clearly now *Didi*, except that I was screaming like a savage. Later the children also started shouting. Then, people living in other houses, some distance away, must have seen from their rooftops and joined the commotions, or else the shouts distracted the man. The child fell and rolled down the slope and man got away, rushing up the slope.

Shakun was panting with agitation. Even I sat there, rooted as if frozen.

The two men sat down on opposite ends of a *charpoy* when they returned after seeing Manoj off! My husband was silent as usual, preoccupied, albeit a little disturbed. What was disturbing was my brother's quietness, his utterly dejected silence after myriad failed efforts? His elaborate escarpment had been reduced to rubble.

All his jokes, his jests and memories of the lisping past that had come with peals of laughter – he now stood forlorn like a scared child, punished to stand in a corner for no fault of his.

I broke the silence, forcing myself to get out of the depression, also trying to cheer up Shakun, "Look Shakun, you are the one that's the most unnerved. You have to be the first to think and convince yourself that nothing will go wrong."

"God has saved us from mishaps so far *Didi*, but living with the constant dread something unimaginable or terrible happening is a dreadful existence. You cannot imagine it."

Startled, I looked at my husband.... he had said something similar about the happenings in our town, "The fear of the possibility of dying, writhing...."

It was as if each person's entire life were relegated to the same level.... I, Shakun, brother, children, ours, theirs, everybodys...everyone in the grip of this mortifying terror.

"*Didi!*" Shakun said imploringly, "Please tell my husband to forget his ambition of having his own little house now. What kind of a house is this where we don't have a moment's comfort or peace. Do you know that there is a liquor shop hardly two *furlongs* from here? Imagine a country liquor shop here and the house of a disreputable smuggler on the other side of the railway-line. Right before my eyes, the police caught a boy carrying packet of *hashish* and thrashed him so badly that he lay there for hours, soaked in blood, writhing in pain. Please tell him why shouldn't we return to that rented pigeonhole.. where we may be deprived of sunshine and light, but at least this terror, this fear...."

"And *Didi*," suddenly my brother spoke, flushing, as if announcing a momentous decision, "Please explain to her that it is absolutely impossible for us to return now to the old house in the street. All my money, including a loan, has been sunk in this house. Even if I want to, I will be unable to mobilise an advance, or '*pagari*' nor will the old house or any other new one be available now...therefore, I will live here comfortably and peacefully, or should I say, I will try to live here in comfort and peace. This Shakun will have to make the same effort because there is no other choice."

"It is not that I do not understand what she says – I have done all that I could. Only for her sake do I exchange greetings with that low and depraved scoundrel Bhurelal... in fact he is out of town for the last 3-4 days, otherwise every other day he plants himself on a chair here for hours and talks rubbish. Sometimes he even spreads out on the *charpoy* and I tolerate him, just nod and go 'heh heh heh', unable to say anything to him. How can I tell you how changed, rather, how fallen I find myself? Do you think I living for myself? by my own free will? in my own way? I am living only for the solace of Shakun and the children.... Ask her, though, how many Bhurelals shall we fall at the feet of, wagging our tails, and how much further our conscience will permit this? Ask her which city in India, or in the world, would she like to live in; which one would be totally safe for her – and I will sell myself to provide her a ticket for that city. And when she insists, again and again, that we return to that stinking, suffocating house in that narrow street, ask her whether knives have not been drawn or bombs not confiscated there. Did she feel absolutely relaxed and safe in that lane? Has she forgotten all that so quickly?"

"Please tell her, *Didi,* that she must find within herself the art of living. If she wants to live...forever embroiled in this torment and torture...."

It seemed my brother was beginning to faint with exhaustion as he spoke; the three of us watched this new face of his head and I turned to Shakun.

"And the most important thing, Shakun, is that you have the capacity to fight these situations. The way you risked your own life, forced the man to abandon the child and saved its life, was something no other woman could have done. If there were someone else in your place, she would have hidden away – frightened or thinking that it was not worth risking one's life for."

A flame lit up in Shakun's eyes for a moment, then died. "But *Didi*, whoever hears the story says that you should not have shouted. Or created a scene. You should have kept quiet. Now those people will try all means to threaten and harass you. They have even seen your house.... be very careful about your children. Now those people have found a target...."

"They are mules, all of them; First-degree cowards, worthless and impotent – all of them" my brother lost his temper and screamed. Then as if cowed down by his own echo, he said in a voice deep in despair, "Maybe I don't have the right to call anyone a coward or doubt his manliness, *Didi*, because I find a strange fear creeping inside myself all the time. It is not the fear of some stones or brickbats, of flood or liquor-vend, of daggers or pistols... it is fear of the dread that lives in Shakun's eyes.... I cannot tell you how wary and frightened I am of this dread that has settled in her eyes."

"I have tried my best to help Shakun get better of her fear, but failed. And failing, time and again, I now find myself so weak and useless that each time I have to face her eyes, I curse myself. Her eyes remind me of my own ineffectiveness; make me even weaker. I am no longer that Biru of the old, *Didi*. In fact, I am not even a shadow of my old self now...only a cowardly worthless failure, so small in defeat; to have lost the very essence of life in one's own life time."

And then my manly, life-loving brother placed his head on my shoulder and convulsed, whimpering like a child.

There were tears in my brother's eyes, tears unbearable to me. Something burned inside me and I turned towards Shakun, only to be frozen in shock. Shakun stood there numbed, petrified. There was a new kind of dismay on her face, a petrifying fear; the sight of tears in the eyes of her beloved mate, husband, man and, above all, her inseparable friend.

Then slowly that fear and dismay was overcome by an infinite regret...and through her repentance came her laugh...of atonement; of the conquest of the self, of self-realisation....

And suddenly, not knowing what else to do, Shakun picked up the pack of cards and tugged at my brother's drooping shoulders with an entreaty, "Come, let us at least play cards inside. Are you listening?"

"All four of us..." and she smiled, regenerating an eternal confidence in my brother's eyes.

Oh! Shakun looked so beautiful when she smiled.

□

2

PERHAPS...

I, a semi-old grandmother.... I thought I would find the small mansion also old, mottled, sad and faded. But I found it waiting anxiously for me to open it, and spread out its old box of memories and gossip.

What has faded? Only the writing on the wall of the inner room, written at the time of my marriage, "*Shri Ganeshay Namaha,*." And also faded were the paper festoons tied to the arches of the mansion. These paper cuttings made welcoming sounds at the lightest breeze, saying, "We are still here, preserving small clippings of past memories."

The marauding gang of grandchildren has come with me. They roam in the mansion, searching its nooks and corners. They are most eager and inquisitive.

"Did you live here? In this mansion, Grandma? When you were our age?"

"Oh, did it belong to your father?" *Not did, it still does!*

"Many years have passed since then?"

"Shall I guess? A hundred, isn't it Grandma?" The youngest child Chillu wants to impress by calling out the highest number he knows.

"Silly, even Grandma is not a hundred years old." All the children started laughing uproariously, falling on each other.

"Aren't you fifty-eight years old, Grandma?" asked Mouli Didi, who was studying in Class III, the eldest amongst the children, impressing the other children with her knowledge. Then, while putting her victorious arms around my shoulders, she asked, "How many years have passed, since you were here?"

A very difficult question! A most difficult calculation!

That is why the gang of shouting children departs to raid the mansion once again. How does one count the years gone by? It seems as if a century has gone by. As if an entire lifetime has passed....

"You liar," the old mansion pinches my cheek, "Nothing has passed by, everything is as bright as a chandelier."

"Within you?" I ask the mansion.

"No, within you also—also in this old city, this old lane; this mansion...."

The mansion was merging the past with the present as if they were old friends teasing each other. That unpaved, earth-filled corner of the courtyard used to have the *Paarijat* tree! The rest of the courtyard was tiled. In the middle of the corridor, a lantern used to burn. When it was put out, we were scared of ghosts.

"Did the ghosts really visit you?" asks Chillu, with his eyes wide and round.

The young Mouli Didi says, "You idiot," and kisses him on the head.

In the ground in front of mansion, there was a *Neem* tree. It is still there! Look at it! The terrace used to be covered with its berries. In fact, now the ground in front of the mansion is so covered with the wholesalers' sheds that it is difficult to recognize it as our old *Neem* tree.

The temple and its platform, at the corner of the street, has also been extended now, and is painted with yellow and red paint. Only the *Hanumanji* within is the same as before.

Every Tuesday evening they used to have a prayer at this temple. Do they still have it now? Perhaps!

The priest used to ring the bell, and walk round the *Hanumanji* with lighted *aarati.*

The aura of light and the burning flame of *aarati....* The heap of faces in the crowd surrounding the *aarati* glowed brightly in the light of the flame. After the *aarati* was over, the priest would extend the plate of *aarati* towards everyone, chanting holy prayers to *Hanumanji.* The offerings given to *Hanumanji* on Saturday and Tuesday were *kevda* and cardamom-flavoured *laddoos* or *pedhas.*

"Please offer this *prasad* on behalf of my son, he has passed the college examination with first class," said someone to the priest. "Son, touch the feet of *Panditji.*"

The flame of the *aarati* stops. Blushing face. "God bless you, my son. May all success and progress be yours." The flickering light of the flame. The face in the light continues to blush.

The people gathered come forward, thump his back and congratulate him.

I tiptoed in that crowd to see him. Let me see who is the other person, who has got first class! No, I do not know him! It seems that he is not from our street. Anyhow, you have come first in your class; I am very happy about it. You certainly must be a good boy! All the boys in our street are duffers. Yes, I have also ranked second in my class. Just three marks lower than Sunayana, who stood first. Just because of Maths. I was in tears, but hid it from the others.

What can I do? I do not like Maths. Anyway, now that I have grown up, I force myself to solve Maths problems. But when I was young, Mannu Uncle used to tease me until I cried, saying, "Look here, Maddhu, I will teach you a way to learn the tables by heart!" Then he would sing a meaningless ditty, rhyming with the tables of 13. What an idiotic ditty, but everybody would laugh and then I cried. That was because I was very young then.

Now?

Now my skirts were becoming shorter, my plaits were getting longer. My *chacha* (paternal uncle) advised that I wear full-length dresses to cover my knees. Mother accordingly gave me a *salwaar-kurta* with a long *chunni* too. Mannu uncle again started teasing, "The small pony one foot tall, has a tail two feet long." It is *chacha's* whim, "Maddhu is still so young! You have given her such a long *chunni* to wear."

"Don't tell me!" said an *Aunt*, "a girl of her age from our locality ran away with a Muslim."

"Oh! He must have taken her away to convert her to his religion! We have heard so many such stories of the settling of personal scores!"

"No, No," the elder sister said, "You unnecessarily doubt everything! Don't tell me Hindus are pure as snow. Mussalmans are more gentle and cultured compared to Hindus."

"Stop it, you are talking about Hindus and Mussalmans for no reason. What we are talking about is taking care of such teenage girls."

"Why don't you talk of taking care of boys?"

"Don't argue unnecessarily my child, go and say that to parents of boys, OK?"

"Yes, Aunty, tell me, then what happened to that girl?"

"Then what? The parents' faces were blackened, no, tarred. They were ridiculed and nobody even looks at them in our town!"

"That was as it should be! *Arrey*, did she not get anybody from *Brahmin, Kshitriya* or *Baisya*?"

"Grandma, Grandma!" the gang of children came shouting, "Daddy and Mummy told us that they are going out for some work again!"

My son and daughter-in-law are running around. Court, Office, Buyer, Broker, Agreement, Sale Deed, Stamp Paper, Documents. My elder son insisted, "Mother, you come along too. As it is, you would know this better. Chhota is not able to come. In fact, he is sending away his troupe of children with us! And brokers and buyers will probably respect your age."

"Yes, Yes, Grandma, please come, let us all go together," the children insisted.

Future, Past and Present.

Infancy, childhood, and old age.

From the lantern of the old corridor to official agreements.

All of these together and with me!

Wrong, you silly one! I was not talking about you! Why would you be with me!

Mine and yours are two parallel lanes, never meeting each other!

Yours must definitely be some lane at the back of the street. Let it be, what do I care? You also have not seen my mansion. You probably did not know, I think!

Yes! That is what everybody thinks; but I know you do know my lane, where I live.

Shall I reveal how you know?

One day, while I was returning from school, you were walking behind me, busy chatting with your friend! Perhaps that day you had to go to the football ground, through this lane. What else could be the reason otherwise?

That time, when I ran toward our entrance, right then and there, I knew that you had definitely seen my mansion, if not me.

Why would you look at me, if at all? You are a nice, good boy. Always ranking first or second in the class. I too am a nice girl; why should we look at each other?

We should not look at each other, right?

Because my *Aunts* were talking about Manjula *Bhabhi's* sisters—

"All of them are tarts. All dolled up with powder, bindi, eye-shadow, mascara; they are always smiling at one and all! Staring at everybody. Sooner or later, Manjula's sisters will tarnish the family's name. All the time they eye and laugh from the window, at the passers-by. Listen, why should the girls stare at boys like this? Tell me, is it not frivolity?"

I heard this, and closed my eyes in shock so that I could not see you. But tell me, what could I do at the shop of Pyaare Mohan? I had gone there to buy graph paper. I counted the money and was handing over it to the shopkeeper, and then I saw you reflected in the many mirrors kept in the shop's showcase, asking Pyaare Mohan for a geometry case.

Yes, I saw you properly—I mean, you were there to be seen—you were smiling too, not at me, but while talking to Pyaare Mohan.

I ran away, as I did not know what to do. But I was thinking, you were looking at flying braids on my back, and were smiling softly. How nice it was that you did not see me face-to-face!

Definitely, you also must have heard from your *Aunty*.....

"Saw that son of that woman from Bhopal! Always roaming on the road, whistling along, combing his hair and wearing narrow bottom pants! He has failed thrice in XII standard! I don't think he will study further. The son of that *Indorewali* is okay in studies but is a rogue, he wears foreign scents from now itself! Tell me, is this the way a boy from good family behaves? Studious boys do not have time for all this nonsense nor know the streets where the beautiful girls stay."

Yes, it is very true! I talked about you looking at my mansion, only because everybody, who passed by our mansion, would look at it and say to others, "This mansion belonged to Mr. Shukla. He had built it with style, but within four months after completion, the poor fellow died in his sleep. He was a great man! Died very young, had small children. His relatives are helping his family now."

I hear steps climbing up the staircase. "How was your day, *Grandma*? Were all the children good?"

"Shall we tell? We were detectives!" shout the children.

I am startled and disturbed.

My son and daughter-in-law are also worried. It seems the deal was not happening. They were not able to sell the mansion. I had believed that everything would be finished once and for all. But the sly buyers were thinking that we are in need for money and, hence, had only to say, "Reduce the price, Sir. It takes a lot of money to repair old mansions. The structure has become old and outdated. Nobody wants to live in old mansions. All these arches and chandeliers are only for emotional satisfaction."

"*Daddy, Daddy! Grandma* says there used to be a lantern in the corridor and ghosts used to visit there on dark nights."

"How is it possible? You were not born at that time!" My son tapped Chillu's cheek. Immediately, the other children started teasing Chillu, "You are a ghost, ghost!" and running away from him.

"Quiet! Such noise, and you tell us you were wellbehaved!"

"No, No, we were all right throughout the day! Ask *Grandma*!"

Not throughout the day, throughout life! Remember, once I was standing in the outer balcony and suddenly saw you passing by in the street below. I could not believe it! May be it was someone who resembled you—but no it was you.

Why are you passing by this street, this lane? Let me see where you are headed.

But oh! What is this? You are entering the gate of my mansion! My breathing became uncontrolled. What if you knocked upon our door?

Sure, there was a knock on our door. Everyone was away for a marriage in Civil Lines. Mother said, "Maddhur, have a look, who is at the door?" With trembling legs, I went down the staircase. I opened the door and right in front of me, there you stood.

You... You, what should I do? Must I say something? But I stand stunned, frozen, with downcast eyes, looking at the floor. Is it possible to see your image in the floor!

"This is an invitation to my elder brother's wedding. My father has sent me to give it here!"

I have grasped the wedding card. Now what? I must say something or at least look at you. Nothing of that sort happened. I could not even stand there. Tears came to my eyes and, not being able to think any further, I turned back and ran into the house... fast, hurdling up the staircase... as if I myself was running after me and trying to stop me... "Are you mad! Stop! Why are you running away! Stop, Maddhur!"

But I reached the top floor and was breathless.

Like a good girl!

I don't know how long you stood there—surprised or sad—I do not know.

But why would you be sad? As if you had come running only for me. You had only thought to help your father by distributing the invitation cards in your locality. That's all!

Like a good boy!

How stupid of me! I did not even ask your name! Don't you ask the name of strangers visiting your house?

Upon coming upstairs, I quietly gave the card to the mother. I was breathless after running up the steps. "Who has given this?" asked my mother.

"A boy!"

"Was he from the Mathurs?"

"I don't know; I forgot to ask."

"My child, you should have asked him to sit. How could you make this mistake? Anyway, you attend the wedding with the gift." Everybody knows that after father's death, mother never attends any functions. Mother insisted that I wear pearl earrings in my ears, a *sharara-kurta* (special dress for marriages), a pearl necklace, and placed a gift in my hand.

Today, I was permitted to put a small *bindi* on my forehead. I silently went and stood in front of the mirror. I took one look at myself and blushed heavily. Then I asked the mirror hesitantly, "All this is not bad, is it? I am still a good girl, am I not?"

The mirror said lovingly to me, "By all means! All girls wear good dresses and beautify themselves. They scamper, dance, laugh and play in a wedding ceremony.

You should also dance, sing, and laugh at the wedding hall. There is nothing wrong in it."

The mirror was right! The girls were all dressed up in satin *shararas*, and they tied bells to my ankles and insisted that I dance!

Then there was a public demand that I dance to a popular song. "She is a very good dancer, just like a rubber doll," they said.

With accompaniment of the drum and the girls' singing, I started dancing with twists and twirls. People started clapping to the rhythm. A mood of festivity was set and the women started showering me with rupee coins.

And you! I had seen everything while dancing. You were smiling all the time, while carrying dishes full of sweets.

What were you thinking and smiling? Since you were not watching! Did you realize that I was dancing only for you, to apologize for the mistake I made when I left you standing at the door and ran away! *A good girl is permitted to do this small thing, isn't she?*

"Mouli, Tannu, Chillu... Sorry we are late! What have you been doing?" "*Daddy*, we were all playing our games." "Hope you did not trouble *Grandma*?" "Ask Grandmother, we did not disturb her at all! All day we played *Aankh Michouli* (Blindman's Bluff)."

I too had played the same game.

My son was very happy. And my daughter-in-law was brimming with joy.

"You know, *Mummy*, we got a very honest and very nice buyer, exactly what we wanted. A highly respected buyer. He had come to grandfather's mansion. The price is very good too. Rahul just blurted out, 'Eighteen lakhs,' expecting him to bargain. But the buyer just accepted that price. He stays somewhere in this area. Rahul, what did he say his name was?"

"Mummy, we have invited him over this evening for tea. I told him *Mummy* will be happy to meet him!"

I thought you must at least see the person to whom your mansion is going. "But *Mummy*, you would have been happy to meet him!"

Yes, I do see, I do hear!

There were songs at my marriage. The songs resound in my mind. While listening to those songs, I wondered whether my wedding invitations were given to everyone in my locality. Whom should I ask? Whom should I tell? Somebody should go!

Let us gather the scattered, shredded pieces of time, moments! Gather and see, if from these pieces emerges the picture of a "good girl" and a "good boy."

Perhaps....

□

3

Homeless

The scorching wind tore through the eucalyptus and casuarina trees, stripping them of their dried leaves. The lawn was soon covered with a bed of withered leaves and dust. The rose bushes looked shrivelled. A strange gloomy atmosphere.....all was still except for this harsh wind blowing through the windows.

She closed the windows, drew the curtains and stood for a while near the window, lost in thought. A quiet, strangely eerie afternoon such as this one was bearable once in a while, but how on earth was one to endure the coming weeks, months, years?

Of course the afternoons of the month of *'chaitra-baisakh'* had always been like this. She had seen so many in her lifetime but never any like this one. Or perhaps there never had been much time to dwell on the weather. Her two small children had occupied most of her time. She had to listen to their happy prattle, solve their quarrels and, of course, those stories to lull them to sleep. How often she'd fallen asleep telling them stories. And how naughty her sons were. Why, Dhiru, the little one, would quietly slip away in the afternoon to play in the garden and steal the fruit from the '*falsa*' tree. She wouldn't even know he had slipped away till the servant brought the little fellow back... A hundred chores, day after day...drinking water to be constantly replenished in the '*surahi*'...water to be sprinkled in the courtyard and *verandah*, to cool the atmosphere... aniseed and black pepper to be ground for *Babuji's* favourite drink, '*thandai*'....

She opened her prayer book, read a couple of verses and closed it again. The wind wrenched her *saree* and other clothes from the clothes-line in the *verandah* and blew it in. She stooped to pick it up, folded it and put it away on the rack. What next, she wondered? She opened her little bag, removed the prayer beads and began to count them...one...two...three. Soon sleep overcame her.

She woke up with a start. Oh God! What was the time? Surely it was not 4 p.m. already? Everything was quiet except for the buzz of the aircooler. The bedroom door was still shut, that meant her son and daughter-in-law were still asleep,

She made her way to the living room. Her husband had fallen asleep on the armchair. The glasses were still perched on his nose and a book lay half open on his tap. She put the book away and was about to remove the glasses when he woke up.

"Oh, it's you? What's the matter? Couldn't you sleep?"

"I did, for a while. It is far too hot. Did I wake you up?"

"No, my dear. I wasn't really sleeping, just dozing."

"Shall I make some *sherbet*?"

"Why don't we have some tea instead? By the time you make it, Rajan and *Bahu* will have woken up."

She went to the kitchen and discovered that there was no kerosene in the stove. Even as she began to fill it up, the kerosene bottle slipped from her hands and crashed to the floor.

Rima, her daughter-in-law, came rushing in. Quickly she bent down and hurriedly began to mop up the mess. "Oh, it's you!" remarked Rima.

She smiled guiltily, "Your father-in-law is awake. I thought of making tea by the time you both got up..."

"Tea at this unearthly hour! Couldn't you have waited till the evening? Jamna would have come and made it in a little while...."

"But it is already four. I was dying for a cup of tea."

"So, you thought you'd help yourself," laughed Rima and walked off.

No, Rima hadn't meant anything, she'd just laughed, there was nothing to feel bad about surely, but she wondered why the tears stung her eyelids.

From the bedroom snatches of their conversation floated to her.

Rima was telling Rajan, "That was your mother in the kitchen, making tea, at least trying to. God knows why she wanted tea in this hot weather. You know, she's not exactly young, so the bottle slipped and fell...."

"Couldn't you explain to her then? If she wants her tea earlier, maybe we could ask Jamna to come in a bit earlier." "So, you think I was forcing her to come to the kitchen? I'd rather, she stayed away. She makes more work for all of us if she comes, she's always upsetting something or the other. I tell you these old people...."

Old people. Was she really that old? Incapable of any work? Till they moved in here, hadn't she been efficiently running her own household—the cooking, cleaning, washing.... *Babuji* had never complained. Her cooking, unlike Jamna's, was always just right with the correct proportion of salt and spices.

Their conversation floated back once more.

Rajan was saying, "How lovey-dovey they are. She constantly wants to sit with *Babuji*. Imagine, at their age too! Have you noticed *Babuji's* behaviour. He insists on washing his own clothes, doesn't let her do any work. And he keeps asking her how she is feeling, if she has taken her medicine...." Rajan broke off with a smothered laugh.

Her husband put down the empty cup and wondered where his wife had gone. Then he changed his mind, put on his glasses and began to read the paper. He thought, 'I wonder whether I've ever read the newspaper as thoroughly as I've done in the past year and a half....'

They had come to live with their son a year and a half after he had retired. Rajan till then had been regularly sending them money every month. Suddenly one day, his letter arrived, asking them to come and live with them permanently. They could rent out their house, he'd written. He'd seemed genuinely concerned that his mother was doing all the work single-handed. He was also worried about their health. His job did not permit him to look them up as frequently as he'd have liked to....

Their friends and neighbours had agreed with Rajan. "What he says is correct. You must go and live there. Here *Babuji* has to do some of the outside work, there you'll have a battalion of servants waiting on you. After all, Rajan is a senior government officer. And then his wife is such a nice girl. Rajan's mother will be able to lord it over there like a queen. And the best part is that Rajan still cares for his old parents, not like other sons nowadays...."

Only the *gurkha's* wife had commented, "Of course, you will live well in your son's house. But it won't be your own. You will have to live as he wants you to....

But I guess it will be more comfortable, also it seems ungracious to refuse...."

There had been endless discussions between husband and wife. The idea of giving up their house killed them with nameless doubts and fears. But why? Wasn't Rima a nice girl? She was, yet...? Why was there a strange fear clutching them? Weren't they their own children? Fine, Rajan may be a highly placed officer but so what, to them he was still their little boy....

"I've done the reservations" Her husband's voice sounded as if someone had brought a hammer down on her. Suddenly there was a flurry of activity. Oh, these material possessions of man! So much, yet all necessary for the running of a household. Clothes, utensils, pestle and mortar, strainers, the *'puja saman'*, the *'tulsi chora'* for *Ramnavmi*, the tiny swing and image of Lord Krishna for *janamashtami*.... Oh God, did they have to leave everything behind? Rajan had written "Please tell *Amma* not to bring everything. Our house is well equipped." She hesitated, and then quietly added the *'puja saman'*, the Krishna idol and the brass *'lota'* they'd picked up from Rameshwaram. She remembered their visit to Rameshwaram, where they had taken a holy dip in the sea and offered thanksgiving to the Lord for his plentiful bounty. Rajan had just got his job then....

Rajan had come to the station to receive them, along with two servants. His gaze took in the baskets, trunks and bundles on the platform and he said, "*Babuji*, hadn't I written to you to restrain *Amma*. My God! she seems to have brought all this ancient stuff with her."

Her husband gave an embarrassed laugh. "You know how these women are. They just don't seem to understand. Don't worry. We'll manage somehow...."

The servant showed them their room. Rima took one look at the luggage and laughed, "You really seem to be a walking museum! God knows what the servants will think looking at all this junk." She spotted the brass 'lota' and quickly hid it out of sight. Her mother-in-law looked at her mutely, unable to protest.

All their luggage was put away in the loft so that they couldn't reach it easily. A couple of times she thought of asking Rima for her old possessions which were so dear and familiar to her, in fact, she had asked once or twice but no one had paid any attention. She remembered with anguish all she had been forced to leave behind in her own home. But now it looked like she had lost a great deal more than just her possessions. An irreplaceable loss....

Babuji had managed to adjust himself as best as he could. He tried to make friends with the neighbours. Every morning he would go for a long walk, often calling out to his wife, "What are you doing now? Come on, let's go for a walk, or maybe we can read our prayer books...." A few times he'd even commanded his son to join them, but Rajan's curt reply had stopped him from asking again. He'd said, "I've a meeting to attend. Anyway I've plenty of time before I start going for walks and reading prayer books."

One day, her daughter-in-law in a sugary-sweet voice had told her, "*Maaji*, please tell *Babuji* to recite his daily prayers quietly. He says them so loudly, even the neighbours can hear. After all, God is everywhere, you needn't shout yourself hoarse surely?"

She was stunned at Rima's request, but managed to console herself. Of course, Rima was right. Why she herself had felt that *Babuji* was saying his prayers rather loudly? What would the neighbours think? Poor Rajan and Rima, it must have been so embarrassing for them. And one must learn to adjust oneself and live the way others do, she told herself sternly.

She looked out of the window and saw Rajan and his father chatting comfortably on the lawns, sipping tea. It sure felt good to see father and son together.

Rajan finished his tea and stood up. He hesitated for a minute and then spoke up. "*Babuji*, after you return from your evening walk, please come into the house and stay indoors. I am expecting some friends over. Most of them smoke and also drink, so if you could..." his voice trailed away, and then calling out to the servant, he told him to clean the car as they were going out.

"*Maaji*, we are going out and will eat out. When Jamna comes back with the baby, please give her the milk," said Rima.

She looked at the dust that the speeding car left in its trail for a while and came to the lawn to see her husband relaxing with a book.

"They've left."

There was no reaction. "Can I see what you are reading," she asked, "Is it a new book?"

"No, just the *Ramtirth Granth*."

She lapsed into silence, again. All was quiet again. Then again she spoke, "What shall I make for you? I think I'll make yam curry. You love it, don't you?"

"No, forget it. I don't seem to be able to digest it any more."

"Then some plain vegetable, and maybe a little '*kheer*'."

"*Kheer*? No, not right now. You can make some when Rajan and Rima are here."

She fell silent again. She recalled the happy days when they were in their own home; how he used to enjoy her cooking the thick '*parathas*', the '*alu baingan sabji*', and once in a while the '*makhaane ki kheer*', when they were happy about something. And now....

Darkness descended around them. She got up and went quietly and sat next to her husband. Gently she asked, "It's been so long. Can we go home, just once?"

"Home?" Her husband's eyes lit up, but almost immediately dimmed again, "But we have rented it out, remember? Why, is something the matter?"

"No, No, nothing really. It is just that. I feel it has been ages since we left home."

"I know, I know, but what is the use of going for just a few days?"

"You are right," she sighed deeply.

A telegram arrived the next day to inform them about the arrival of their younger son Randhir. Rajan fetched him from the station at ten O'clock. Randhir bent down to touch his mother's feet and asked, "How are you *Amma*? It is good you've come here. Now you too can order everyone around, like *Bhaiyya* does."

Her husband laughed and said enthusiastically, "Yes, there are plenty of people coming here everyday. The servants, the orderlies, the VIPs...."

Rajan stubbed his cigarette and said dismissively, "Actually he is just exaggerating. There is nothing so fantastic about this job. Times are difficult for everyone, the prices, the many difficulties. I'd love to send my daughter to a boarding school in Nainital next year but...."

Dinner was over, Randhir was about to go to his room, when Rajan stopped him. "Where are you going? Why don't we sit around and chat for a while? Anyway we sleep rather late." Then he looked at his father. □

4

A Woman's Feats

I'm of average height and build, an almost-beautiful woman; you can call me a lady; well educated, cultured and intelligent, perhaps even say that I'm an intellectual. I'm also married to an almost-dignified, handsome and healthy man of five feet eleven inches, and am the wife of a husband who is a man of few words, and even those—uttered softly... gently.

Kids? Of course. Daughter and sons, born, fortunately, in a timely and convenient manner; kids that have grown into precocious and obedient young adults who complete their homework on time. Fortunately, we have adequate means to ensure that this little caravan of one husband, two domestic maids and three children can skip along the path of life, feeling happiness at every bounce. In other words, the children's studies, after-school classes and extracurricular activities, midterms and finals, all take place in a convenient and organized manner. That's us—convenient and organized.

My husband gives me what I want to run the house; he lets me go wherever I want to go. He never interferes or stops me, doesn't even question what I do. When I ask him to accompany me, he comes along; and doesn't when I don't ask him to. Our food is also always simple and wholesome. If, occasionally, I repeat the dishes too often, I murmur apologetically, "Sorry," he responds extremely softly, "It's alright."

In other homes, I've seen enough of calamity-causing, seismic husbands who have convulsions because either the salt is a little less or the chili, a little more. First, there's the earthquake and then the aftershocks of mollified offerings. It takes a good hour or two to deal with the whole year's casualty calendar. But in my home, I swear, this hasn't happened even once, which is why our friends and neighbours say my husband is no ordinary man—he's a saint.

We have one colour TV, two phones and get three newspapers. The newspapers are scanned before and after office; the TV is usually turned on when he's home. He has no favourite channels or shows. Irrespective of what is on, he watches it; whatever the subject, he doesn't get upset or change the channel, ever. He's never in a dilemma of what to do with his time. It passes, on its own, comfortably enough: otherwise most people have a full-fledged workout thinking of how to spend time, save time. No such indecisiveness pervades my husband's world. He is the ideal solution of these problems, which is exactly why our friends and neighbours say my husband is no ordinary man—he's a saint.

Oh but what can I say about myself? Just thinking about me is embarrassing. I have no wisdom or quietude to match his saintliness. The more angelic he gets, the more bent and misshapen I become. If I laugh, I chortle loudly, splitting my sides, and when I cry, it's a monsoon deluge, showing no sign of ceasing. I function on a short fuse; even the smallest thing gets me fuming and frothing, at my saint-like husband, without a syllable being uttered. I'm well aware on such occasions that it's all my fault but he, in his quiet and gentle way (without knowing, hearing or understanding why I'm furious), says, "It's OK," or, "So sorry..." Our neighbours say that to date they haven't heard his voice raised. It's true; when I haven't heard it inside the house, how can anyone sense it outside?

Take, for instance, a Sunday; if I see him leaving, no matter how hard I resist, I can't help asking, "Are you going somewhere?"

"Yes."

"Where?"

"Out."

"Out, where?"

"I was to meet someone..."

"Who?"

"You don't know him."

"OK. When will you return?"

"I may come back soon, or it may take time."

See, didn't I tell you earlier—soft-spoken, man of few words. Tell me, is this any excuse to fret or hit the roof? No, right? But I don't miss the opportunity to start an argument. To hell with his equanimity when I want to squabble! One time, I got down to it pretty fast. I said, "You never even talk to me. All the time, it's newspapers, TV, computer, phones."

He kept the newspapers aside, turned off the TV and said in matured, measured tones, "I'm sorry. OK, tell me what should I talk about?"

Tell me, don't you think he is compliance personified? He is asking *me* to tell *him* what he should talk about with me.

But when it came to suggesting something, my mind drew a blank. Nervously, I tried to come up with a topic I could introduce but no luck. I got increasingly anxious; he was waiting for me and I couldn't come up with anything.

Faltering, I said, "*Arey*, if there's nothing else, tell me about your day in office. So many big things must have occurred. Tell me about them."

"Yes, sure," he said and tried to recall. Then, in an even tone, he began telling me as I prepared to listen attentively. When he reached the office in the morning, his peon, Pyarelal, had gone off, like always, to get tobacco leaves from another peon, Kamta. The woman at the switchboard came in late. By ten thirty, the packing department was on 'go slow' mode because of which the consignment that should have been loaded by three-thirty was still being loaded till five-thirty, in fact, five-forty-five. The trucks had to wait longer. Tensions between the packing department and the loading people remained high because of all this. Cashier Baruah extended his vacation and several bills couldn't be reimbursed. Makhija, the assistant at the chemical lab, was again caught stealing some cultures. Meanwhile, there was a power cut for an hour-and-a-half...the tanker at Rehmatganj brokedown. There was a budget meeting from three-thirty...and then I hear, "Should I talk more or is this enough?"

His inquiring tone wrenches me out of my torpor. *Uff!* I had forgotten that I had asked him to talk. He was giving me this long, faithful account of his office drama to oblige me, whereas, I had heard the first two sentences and then drifted off. Who knows, maybe I fell asleep. I hadn't managed to hear or understand much. Isn't this the limit of my impoliteness that first I attack him with demands and questions and then yawn and get distracted while he tries to appease me with appropriate answers. Now he was forced to ask if we should talk some more.

I felt dejected and, to save the situation, said, "Let it be. You must be tired. I'll make some tea. Should I?"

He had turned on the TV once I declined his offer of more conversation, and was watching it serenely. He hadn't heard my question for tea. I waited for a while and then asked again, "Do you want tea?"

"OK, I can have some," he answered, in a quiet voice.

I walked towards the kitchen like a smart and responsible wife; put the pot on the stove. Suddenly, out of a place I didn't know existed, a wave of exasperation rose within me, as if I was having a fit; as if all the functioning rationality was being exploded molecule by molecule; a destructive bulldozer had materialized out of nowhere and was determined to tear down and level all the buildings standing in line like well-behaved school children. It seemed that I was controlling this destructive force and, at the same time, also screaming, all distraught, pleading for the bulldozer to stop. Amidst the internal strife, of the why and how, I could make out some little meaning...

"What does he mean, 'OK, I can have some!' Is he doing me a favour?" Why can't he be like other normal men and simply say, 'Yeah, great, please make some tea. I can use some right now'? Or he could have said, 'Put some ginger and black pepper too, make it really strong and spicy, OK?'

But this line of thinking was pointless, the daydreams obscene, unlawful even...these castles I built in air had come crashing down, wrecked and razed to the ground. What was left, tacked to the detritus, was a sickening, depressing phrase, 'I'll drink some.'

This was the chimera of my private world. Outside, the water on the stove had begun to boil; On the tray, as is our custom, I had arranged the cups and saucers, the sugar and milk pots.

Suddenly, once again, the fit seized me. This time the water was boiling inside me. The flame looked wild, leaping into the air, scorching and searing things it touched. I had no control over my mind or body; the maddened and maddening exasperation had taken charge. I tried to restrain myself but the delinquent part of me threw a spoonful of powdered black pepper into the boiling water along with the tea-leaves and ground ginger.

As he takes the first sip, my heart is pounding inside my head and I forget to breathe. He's going to say something now...now...now. I can't wait any more.

My impatience gets the better of me. "What? What happened? Too much pepper, right? Say...say it...say something!"

"Yes."

I will, my heart to stop pounding as I ask him, "So?"

"It's all right."

"What?!" I can't believe my ears. Now the internal demon is lawless, unmanageable. "All right... how is it all right? Why don't you just tell me honestly that the tea is not just spiced with black pepper but soaked in it? It's damned black pepper soup...and I've made this fiery soup deliberately, so that these glacial walls between you and me crumble; so that the ice melts and water flows, and brings in a wind that ruffles even if it is turbulent; wind, water, ice, storm, thunderous clouds and lightning...all together. Enough of this saintliness! Just a dash, but I want some madness, an irrationality, a reaction. I want this armour of precious metals to crack and the real, alive, breathing man to emerge...."

I keep waiting but the storm doesn't come; no thunder or lightning; no angry clouds or pelting rain. I get up from my seat, feeling remorseful. I hear myself say, "Sorry, I put too much pepper, I'll make it again," and I leave the room with the tea tray.

You don't believe me, do you? Even I was watching, stunned and shell-shocked, my 'angelic', husband and I, drinking tea together, quietly... peacefully.

□

5

The Frock with Yellow Flowers

I had opened the door.... And you stood there right in front of me.

You...that is the stranger of today!

Like any other stranger, you had said, hesitatingly—

"I...am...Kaushal Verma...."

I was also able to respond just like you—

"Yes.... Yes.... Please come in!"

You had come inside. Then a silence with internal vibrations, a state of vagueness and then again you asked hesitatingly, "You.... You are Manu, is'nt it!"

As if a small bell had tinkled. Manu was my name, when I was a very young child.... The name, which perhaps even I had forgotten. Ravi always calls me Manisha or just 'Mani' at the most when engrossed or with love. He says, this Mannu-Vannu sounds totally rustic.

"Yes, Yes...." This time, somehow I collected myself and smiled and then I started winding up of *pallu* of my *saree*, around my fingers.

The stranger, that is...you smiled.

"You have not been, perhaps, able to recognize me, must have forgotten...." *Oof*, these few words and how they have triggered off a silent storm, within me.

Everything is getting topsy-turvy, scattered and a thirty-five-year-old good housewife is watching foolishly....

"No.... I do recognize you.... You...perhaps...."

"Keshi!"

"Yes...." My controlled heartbeats again start scattering away. That too because of a very small, very old acquaintance.... And I wind up such a large length of *pallu* on my finger, that my thirty-five-year-old housewife scolds me.... *Oof!* Let him be Keshi.... So what...?

Apart from knowing a little about this name, how else is he connected to you? From some corner of the world, the man was seen centuries ago.... Neither he was remembered any time nor his name was ever thought of. And since he has appeared today, you have started winding up *pallu* around your fingers.... Like that thousands of names get connected to your life...but as far as I remember, this name can never be connected or written about....

"Yes...absolutely not...." I have surrendered to my thirty-five-year-old housewife and have unfurled the *pallu's* end, wound on the fingers.

Again the Housewife, as per her habit, has started giving me a lesson....

And no idea, why this man has come so suddenly, after so many years....

There must be some motive, some purpose or some work. Ravi and I had discussed that why some Keshi, for no reason, would suddenly remember us and take the trouble to visit us? Definitely he wants to take advantage of Ravi's influential position and status to get some information...some job, recommendation or promotion.... Something or the other must be there. Otherwise for no reason, why Kaushal Verma—or OK—Keshi would come and visit us? Hence, Yes, I have to get rid of him quickly, as usual, as I keep on getting rid of so many riff-raffs.

But the stranger, that is you, continue to say—

"Yu...you... You were very young...when I had seen you...."

"Yes, Yes...." I laughed, because till now I had regained my composure.... "Obviously, you too must have been very young then."

For sure, he is trying to build a rapport before disclosing his purpose and work.... "Yes definitely...but not that young that I would forget everything."

'What...?'

I could not say this... It was just the echo of the question which rose within me. Outwardly, I just laughed and had asked casually—"Is it? What have you not forgotten...?"

"Shall I tell? First of all, you...your frock with yellow flowers on it..."

I...my...frock! I was stunned and paled. This...this stranger, what all is he saying!

As if my eyes had closed, mesmerized, and with a magic spell that frock with yellow-white flower-print is pushing around my neck and I am trying to hide here and there.... Some small heartbeat from within me, escaped....

"And...."

"And the yellow ribbon...."

"Ribbon...."

"Yes...ribbon entwined in two tight plaits...."

I again grasp and crumple the end of *pallu* pressed in my fingers and automatically my fingers caress the two locks of hair, near the ears, as if the feeling of two tight plaits still remained there.... My lips get lightly pursed. My housewife looks on...worried and perplexed. I am somehow able to speak out in a half-broken sentence....

"No idea.... Yes," I faintly remember that "yellow frock... and that ribbon...."

"But I remember it very well...." You did not laugh this time. As if sunk in some deep thought...right in front of me.

"Many many years have passed, isn't it!"

"For what?"

"For the same, for the marriage of Sunno *Bua*...."

"Yes, there only I saw you...."

"Yes, I too."

"Obviously, absolutely...."

You had laughed. And I was ashamed at this foolish statement of mine. Really it was so...when you had seen, then I too must have seen. Why was it necessary to say it? Is it something one says, at this grown-up age? Unwittingly, I lifted my eyes, to see what and how much smile is there in your eyes.

But what I saw in your eyes were only silken feathers... many of them. I could not collect even a single feather. My eyes had been lowered shyly. You again had moved to the vision of those of yellow flowers.

"In that marriage...do you remember, one evening there was a power-cut for about half an hour, throughout our area...."

"Yes, Yes.... I remember.... Everybody was worried because, in that season of marriages, even the gas-lanterns were not available."

"Candles were lit and then it was decided that, since nothing else was possible, we will play *Antakshari* of songs...."

"Yes, Yes, one group consisted of all gents and boys and the other was of ladies and girls...." I was excited.

"Your group was absolutely bland...mostly girls who used to blush for no reason and sang in shrill voice, after lots of reluctance...."

"But nobody in your group knew the art of singing.... They all made a mockery of music, out of tune and off key.... Totally meaningless songs...."

"So what...? We used to sing immediately, when we got our alphabet.... You people always took a long time and every time you alone had to sing to save your team from defeat...."

"Yes.... What else could I do...?" I said at once, sadly and faintly.

"But how did you know so many songs? My God.... You were so young, still everybody from our group applauded you whenever you sang...."

"Don't know...." I said coyly.... "What I used to sing those days... no idea. God knows what all sorts of songs...."

"I remember the songs you sang that day."

I saw you...my stranger, you were sunk again...pulled you up, laughing jokingly and said, "Hunh, that way I too remember how you once suddenly forgot lyrics of the song you were singing and blushed heavily.... All girls started laughing. In the dark, they whispered to each other—'He is the younger brother of *Aunty* from Bahraich. Forgot the words of the song'...."

"In our group too everyone used to mutter.... See, that one in the yellow frock... She is fighting to win, single-handedly, like the Queen of Jhansi. Otherwise we would have defeated all of them easily, outright...."

"Oh...you remember so much?"

"Yes, I remember everything.... This too, that your party had lost eventually...."

My heart jumped! That loss was really present in my mind till date. This I had come to know today only.... Don't know how I too had reached that end of the century. With head bowed down, I had accepted in a sad voice—"Yes."

"And you had gone to the pillar in the far corner of the courtyard and had stood there and wept silently...."

"No, not at all...."

But my voice was shaking clearly. Accepting my defeat, I had haltingly said, "But how do you know that...?"

"Is it not a strange thing.... While apart from you, till now, nobody else knew that twenty-two years ago, in a pitch-dark night, you leaned against the pillar and had cried...without any sound...on losing one minor event like *Antakshari*...."

"But...how did you know...? It was all dark everywhere!"

"In the dark, I had passed by that pillar carrying a candle."

"Purposely?" *Aah*, how eager I was getting?

"This I will not tell...."

And your voice had trembled like a candle flame.

What had happened to my mind? How was I getting so anxious.... And why?

"Don't know.... Perhaps that time, even I had not known why did I want to go near you, who stood crying near the pillar.... In fact, when my elder brother asked for the pack of playing-cards, before anybody else, I quickly got up before anyone else could decide...."

"But that thing... about my crying..."

I was eager...and...and...shivering.

"Just like that... I had not known why I was feeling bad, right from the beginning itself. I had been thinking that it may so happen that you will cry. In fact.... I had wanted to console you.... Really, I had felt very bad about your defeat...your weeping had made me feel very close to you...."

I looked up with perplexed eyes. This time your eyes did not have feathers in them. They had acquired a clear shining depth, that I thought no canoe could cross.... Therefore, I felt scared and returned back from the shore itself.

But.... But what all this is happening! This stranger, carrying a candle, is leading me along, into unknown dark caves in my mind. With what right? With whose permission? Was he not overdoing? Finally, what does he want? *Uhh!* That could be asked later...let the conversation continue as it is.

"MADAM...GIVE me the money...." It was Ratti, the maid. She was going to the flour-mill with wheat.

I had started giving instructions along with the money—"Ratti, you do not close the tins of flour and rice properly.... This will invite rats.... Close them tightly and you must put some heavy weight, if need be, on the tins...."

"In that marriage also, once you had gone perhaps to the storeroom of grains to bring something and then.... *Oooii!* A loud scream was heard. They all ran and gathered only to find you, badly scared...were clinging to Sunno *Bua* and had been crying and shivering. Then they all laughed and tried to calm you.... You had just stepped on a big rat.... That's all."

You had laughed... Then while looking at me straight in the eyes, you had asked, "Do you remember?"

"Somewhat...." I said coyly.

But no, I had lied! I do remember the complete incident, exactly as it happened.... This too, that on somebody's telling, you ran and went to bring a glass of water to wash my tear-drenched face.... I had told this incident once even to Ravi and children.... But my children or Ravi had not been able to visualize wife or mother in a yellow frock and yellow ribbon. My enthusiasm had cooled down. They could not imagine me as a twelve-year-old, in frock and plaits....

Really I did not know then that I have neatly and safely kept the girl with yellow-flowered frock, of twenty-two years ago, somewhere in some column of my life's story.

Life is strange and curious! It gets divided into as many compartments as the number of people in your life. At times, we do not know which part of our life is gone into which compartment.

I also remember that while leaning against the pillar and crying, I had been thinking why no one had seen that in the pitch-darkness, I was crying... all alone.

That 'Somebody'—who could it be—I had not imagined then. Just a vague feeling existed.

I remember this also, that in that darkness, you had passed by the pillar with a lighted candle. You... a shy adolescent. And I had, in fact, wanted you to take notice of my presence there... But I thought that you did not see me...and passed by without noticing me.

But you had seen me, had noticed my feelings and you kept all that with yourself, neatly and carefully....

I also remember that while singing the songs. I had thought every time for a moment—'Did you like the song...and my singing?'

I remember this also that I had thought if you saw me at the pillar, would you have felt sympathy and nearness towards me?

I remember this too....

And remember this too....

And this too....

No.... I do not remember anything...

"WHAT TIME does Mr. Ravi comes home?"

I suddenly wake up.... Ravi?

"Yes, he comes may come at any time now.... I mean, it is time for him to come...."

"What are you thinking?"

"I, nothing...nothing at all.... Yes, this only that so much time has passed, I have not asked you for even tea or coffee...."

"Yes, let it be.... Seems you offer tea or coffee to people, after a lot of thinking and consideration, isn't it?"

I became controlled again, as you had laughed and said, "But, honestly, I also did not think that you have now grown up so much that you will ask me properly for tea or coffee...."

I myself was behind by twenty-two years....

"I still have not been able to visualize you in the role of a housewife. Per my reckoning you are still that...."

This thought of 'twenty-two years ago' is totally scattering me away. Suddenly, everything has become tangled and complicated.... But at that moment the telephone rings and everything becomes normal.

It's Ravi's phone. Asks about the visitor saying.... "Listen, some urgent work has come up... Is there any problem, if I come late? Will you be able to get rid of him? It is very important that I stay here, please...."

"I...will.... No problem.... OK...."

"Thanks.... And yes how is Bindu's fever?"

"Fever? Yes, don't know.... I have not yet taken the temperature.... Seems it is better...."

"OK...." Ravi has disconnected with relief.

On my return, you ask—"Was it a call from Mr. Ravi?"

"Yes."

"Is he coming?"

"No, some urgent work has cropped up.... He wants you to please excuse him...."

"Oh, but it would have been nice if he had come.... I wanted to meet him."

I raised my eyes with curiosity.

"I heard that he is very good-natured."

"How do you know?" I laughed.

"Just like that! Sometime, somewhere somebody said so..."

Suddenly, I remembered, "And you.... Got married long time back.... Isn't it? Wife...children!"

"Yes, Yes...right." You gave a hearty laugh. "One wife Nirupama, Neeru...and two children, Madhu and Chhavi."

That's all! After this again an unnatural silence. What more and how should I ask?

"It's quite late.... I should leave now."

Again the same storm comes; topsy-turvy floundering.... Somehow I control myself and ask—"But...you did not even tell why you had come? I mean, what work you had?"

You gave me an absolutely guileless look. For a moment, that look had stopped on your face like a calm lake. Do you really... even now, want to know this?

And just one "Bye then!" you said and quickly crossed the door.

I HOLD the door tightly and I am stunned, staring with unblinking eyes.... You are leaving...after bringing to life the naïve past of twenty-two year ago, by a magic spell. After igniting life, you are leaving... I may never be able to see you again.... But I am assured that you have carefully stored me, forever, in the frock with yellow flowers printed on it.

I want to tell that take this piece of my life... so many hours and so many minutes long and so many minutes wide.... It belongs to you.... This piece I am entrusting to you. It belongs only to us...me and you. Nobody else has a share in it.

You find it strange, isn't it? But this is the truth.

And this also...that a twinkling silken curtain is disappearing very slowly. My consciousness, which was like a petal quivering in a storm, is now returning slowly...coming to a thirty-five-year-old pale housewife, standing alone.... The housewife, who stood at the threshold, has not only the end of *pallu* in her fist, but also has kept one end of a century held in it. Yes, this also is the truth.

□

6

The Final Offering

Mother used to tell that he was born on the day India got the Freedom! May be is that the reason he led a life of "Carefree Madness"?

He always used to say—Life is a carnival'. It should be celebrated to the fullest extent. It is a Gift which should be cherished.

A Gift is a gift! May come in whatever form to us! Glittering in the form of heaps of wealth and diamonds or full of love and tiny bits of happiness! Happiness has no measure, i.e., Small or Big! We must celebrate our happy moments whenever we get them.

Truly, he lived his life with this philosophy only.

He used to say we are really not as poor as we consider ourselves! God has given us unlimited wealth of love. Infinite amount of happiness. We can amass it or gift it away the way we want in any quantity!

People used to laugh at his thoughts such as these! They used to call him Crazy! But they loved him, all the same, though grudgingly.

Some people tried—quietly and secretly to live life, as per his style.

To live life as per his style—what was it? Only some good books, melodious music and wandering about (if not travelling on vacations!). He liked wandering in roads, streets and lanes of his town or tramping in nearby temples and localities. If nothing else, he used to sit at a bench in garden, watching the colourful designs of flowers and leaves, different moods of the dome of sky...right from sunrise to sunset. White, Blue, Orange...limitless play of spectrum of colours! And, in the midst of all these, children with shining eyes and wornout clothes chasing the cut loose kites, school-going girls with ribbon-tied hair with joy-filled eyes and blushing smiles!

How one is able to enjoy all these beautiful moments—for free, no ticket charged! Who has stopped us to gather these joys!

Friends used to say, "Our daily struggle to earn our livelihood!" "When you have no food to eat, all these flowers, petals and butterflies become absolutely colourless and useless!"

'No', he used to explain lovingly—the reason is not the 'hunger', it is 'greed' to amass wealth, even robbing from others in the process. Our life is wasted, in this terrifying haste in the rat race to be wealthy! Then how is it possible to celebrate the life! Think for a moment—our needs in life are so few.

Friends used to get annoyed and say, "Do not talk idealistically. Be practical! You have never experienced dread of hunger and pangs of poverty! How will you understand these things!"

"Undoubtedly, decent meal is still a dream for many, which probably will remain always unfulfilled. But let us talk only of people like us, we are well to do and....

The listeners will be abashed and will have nothing to say on this. He will laugh at them but drive home his point—The life will not be so difficult, if we accept our 'Self-deception'. We should be in control of our life!

Really, he controlled his own life. Never took up the jobs which required him to be dishonest! He became a Teacher, so that, at least, he will be able to convey his thoughts to hundreds of students of this generation every year! He will consider that his effort is not pointless, even if a few amongst these hundreds of students are able to understand his thoughts. And it did happen so! His faith, belief triumphed. Soon he had become the most loved teacher of his school!

It was not that he was not insulted in his life! or he was not cheated! or he did not trip! He was indeed shaken, some weak moments did come! He used to then console himself, 'Life is a War'. One has to fight it. And immediately, he used to read that part of autobiography of Mahatma Gandhi in which he was thrown out of first class compartment of the train at Durban.

When he was cheated, he used to call his two daughters and sing in a carefree manner to relieve the pain of being cheated. His daughters used to listen attentively with fluttering eyes and try to understand the song. Wife will laugh and caress his hair lovingly. He called this caress—a broom. It will sweep away the dust and dirt of depressing problems off him.

During all their years together, the wife was sad only once, when, after 4 years of their marriage, a second daughter was born.

He understood it. He understood his duty to console his wife and immediately whispered to wife in a friendly way, "Oh! Since long I had dreamt to have two beautiful daughters. I did not tell it before, afraid that you will be unnecessarily sad if my dream was not fulfilled."

Wife did not really believe this. She said in a dejected tone, "Forget it and start saving from today and improve your bank balance. We need money to marry off two daughters for their dowry."

"Dowry? *Chhi.... Chhi!* Did your father collect money and give dowry?"

Wife surrendered and bowed her head and said, "Not everybody is like you in this world."

"Why? There are people more enlightened than me! Much much better! Do you think that our daughters will require support in the form of dowry to get married? You will see any cultured family will love to have them and will welcome them in their fold. My accomplished and well-behaved daughters will be married off with much respect and honour! And by the time they are grown-up, you will see, "Dowry" system will not be there—this word will be banished from the educated and cultured society. In such enlightened, scientific world, such cheap practices will die by themselves."

Daughters turned out to be bright and talented. There was soft glow of intelligence on their face! Right from the beginning, they continued to get good marks in all the examinations, with distinctions and with scholarships for the highest marks. True, their clothes used to be quite ordinary. Sandals, shoes also ordinary. But the gaudy fashionably dresses did pale against their shining faces, when they alighted from the stage, after receiving numerous awards from the Chief Guest of the function.

But, perhaps, during these days, first time in his life, his mind was beginning to be overpowered by some anonymous sadness and depression. Inspite of convincing himself, he clearly felt that though the burning torch of Awakening and Life is bright, the darkness remains the same, no it is deepening! Everything was drying and was slipping through—whatever he wanted to safely store in his hands. Though the principles and thinking of the people were like, "white starched clothes", their actual behaviour and mentality was like "dirty, wet clothes."

He normally would not have believed, when fathers of marriageable girls—both among the relatives and colleagues, told their disappointing experiences. He was worried and terrified.

It was the first time in his life he felt that he is not able to share his fears and fragmentation either with his wife or with his children! Earlier, he used to forget insufficiencies and insulting experiences in the company of wife and her loving caress through his hair (broom), with the milky laughter of the daughters and with the "Experiments with Truth", by Gandhiji. Now, he was getting suffocated by those very some insults and insufficiencies, silently. He was utterly alone, defenseless and defeated!

He had realised that some nice joys in life were dependent on other persons' whims. Such happiness was possible only due to these persons' mercy.

Really only after some years, whenever he took the marriage proposals for his daughter to the cultured, enlightened families (which were referred to him by his friends and well-wishers), those people blankly asked first about his "Status", instead of talking about education, culture and beauty of his daughters. They wanted all the details about his land, property and wealth. The word "Status" very soon was turned into his "Suitability" and then he used to become helpless and return back home. On the way back home, he used to fabricate some imaginary stories and would tell to his wife and daughters, with hollow laughter, that he did not like the boy at all. How will I place my daughter made of gold into the coalmine of those people?...

Though the daughters used to give a cheerful laughter on his so-called flat refusal, wife used to be silent and would make a sad attempt to caress his head by her weak fingers.

But many times he used to shudder on reading the news related to suicide of girls whose fathers were unable to provide dowry, in the morning Daily Newspaper and like an idiot, he will ask his wife whether the girls have seen today's Newspaper!

Finally, one matrimonial proposal was successful. His daughter's marriage was fixed due to the efforts of one mutual friend. The friend had convinced him to forget principles and to be practical. "You cannot force all other people to be like you or to think like you! You alone cannot claim to change the world, nor you can wait for the world to change. It will be foolish to keep your daughters unmarried because of your thinking! Anyway, now you leave everything to me. I will tell everything about you and your daughters to them, finalise and then I will tell you to go and meet them. I will see that this marriage takes place definitely."

It indeed happened likewise, according to the plan. When he went to them with the formal marriage proposal, the boy's people welcomed him with respect and told him that his friend had given them all the information and details and they were happy and agreeable with them. "Please fix up an auspicious date for marriage and inform us. It will be acceptable to us."

It was difficult for him to believe this. When he accepted the reality, after many days, he again said to himself—"My thinking was correct! Times are changing, bit by bit! In future, perhaps the change will be faster!"

The preparations for the marriage began with a grateful and happy frame of mind. His relatives, friends and daughter's friends came. Festoons, flowers and decorative garlands were put in the marquee and tents.

The boy's people, *"Baraat"* was welcomed with joy and respect. All the auspicious rituals like *"Dwarchar"*, *"Varmaala"*, *"Sindur Daan* and *'Saptpadi"* were carried out, amongst the laughter and teasing. This happiness—keen to feel and express the warmth of newly connected relations! Marriage took place at midnight. The *"Vidaa"* (departure of the girl to the bridegroom's home) ceremony was to take place at the morning.

People started relaxing and resting wherever they found the place for it. Removal of tents/marquee was started by the tent owners.

It was then, at the last hours of the night, the atmosphere started to become one of anxious sharing! The faces of people returning back from the lodging place of *"Baraat"* were wilted and sad. The avoiding of eyes and some cryptic words. All enthusiasm was turned into something slow and stopping! Some inauspicious halt. As if these people were neither able to tell him anything, nor they were able to hide anything!

He was perplexed first and then he was worried. After all, what's the matter? The curiosity to ask or to know anything turned into a sickening worry.

And at the break of dawn, he was shocked, when his worry turned out to be a fact! There was trembling in his limbs and his body seemed to be lifeless—No, how can it be? The friend could not have tricked him. He had totally convinced him and even also the father of bridegroom had promised him.

Though it was told in an unclear and roundabout manner, the desire of groom's father became clear. In high sounding and insulting words, they were trying to say that their politeness was misinterpreted! All the marriage ceremony was carried out in a way much below their expectation and status. Since they demurred and did not ask for anything, it does not mean that....

The mutual friend was not able to attend the marriage and now the Groom's father, when asked about "*Vidaa*", told slimily, that "We had never talked about "*Vidaa*" at all! It is our custom that "*Vidaa*" does not immediately follow after marriage...we will see about it afterwards."

In spite of lot of efforts to control himself, he painfully said, "How can they do like this?"

This..., how is this possible—his words, as if lost in a silent valley! But his relatives and guests were criticizing without mincing their words—"These people are worse than the known tricksters and turned out to be fraudulent."

Somebody must have instigated them....

On this, young lads were outraged—"Can they strip down the decent people on such instigation?" "Don't they have their own mind and brain? Before marriage ceremony, if they had given some such indication, we ourselves would have chased them away from this locality."

Another angry young man blurted out—"You see now! Just now I will go to the camp of Jaddan *"Dada"* and talk to him. These people will understand these stick-wielding goons better and will come to their senses!"

"No,"—he cried with pain, "You people will never do such a thing."

He was troubled by something else.... He knew that Jaddan, a small-time gangster, gives him lot of respect. He bows his head, whenever he sees him, he has never tried to preach Jaddan, only has asked him, "How are you Janardan," on their meeting! Perhaps he must be feeling nice being called by his childhood name—'Janardan'.

Once a close friend of Jaddan was killed in the gang-war. Janardan sobbed and cried when he had gone to offer his condolences. He told only this much—"Masterji, why did you not meet me beforehand! I would have then understood the meaning of winning and getting defeated in life."

And today if he tells him—"Janardan, I have been defeated," my faith in human beings has been stripped off. Now, for some time, let me pawn my "Tracks of Principles" to "Your way of life", only because I am a father and I can stake anything and everything for the sake of happiness of my daughter.

But before this talk with Jaddan, he thought of his daughter. How will he face her? What will he say? That my child! till now, for so many years, I have told you, while sitting together, while swinging you in my arms, while kissing you, whatever I have taught you, on the strength of which I had won your confidence—from tottering footsteps to youth—All that is false, wrong! I am defeated...

No problem. This difference in "Principles" and "Practical life" has always been there! He will not feel sad at all that now he is defeated. He only wants happy life for his daughter, but this calamity will totally devastate the rest of daughter's life.

His principles will remain intact. His habits also. But the daughter's life will be torn and shredded to pieces.

Then what will remain of his fatherhood?

One strong, last incomplete cry!

In his house, there was total grief and sorrow!

"Hypocrites, Rascals! They look honourable from outside, but are always greedy."

"Listen, I have suggested thousand times, send Jaddan and his 4-5 stick-wielding musclemen to them, all their pride of status and boasting will be evaporated in no time!"...

"But, tell me how is the groom silent like a clay doll?"

"Why does he not come forward?"

"Brother, try to understand—when the father has fixed up the marriage, how will he tolerate such foolish intervention of the groom?"

"These are all excuses—being obedient son...all these ideals and discipline—these young boys remember, only at times like this! Down with such behaviour!"

All was faded and sad when the dawn broke. Strings of flower decorations were lifeless and hanging loose. Lines of electric lights, decoration were faded and then extinguished. The holy fire lit in the previous night was also now quiet, with the layer of ashes on it. Only the paper festoons, strung together decoratively, were stirring, as if terrified!

Rest it was silence everywhere!

He sat near the staircase, in the yellow morning sunlight. Alone. He laughed at himself—whether he still hoped for any miracle to take place?

Whether his faith and insistence on "Living life like a celebration" still remained?

His tricked and shattered faith was laughing bitterly—Is it the end of the remains of your sunflower-like faith and belief or....

"Then...shall we inform Jaddan? Yes, call him...to defend the honour of my daughter."

Suddenly, some figure came fast towards him, becoming clear, as it came nearer.

It was Mr. Shuklaji, the neighbour.

Breathless with excitement, he somewhat controlled himself and was uttering half sentences, in bits and pieces—"They, They are coming...get all preparations ready for *"Vidaa."* Immediately."

"Are coming, but how? They were,"...he was in shock and was not able to speak properly.

"I told you! Nothing, Forget everything! No need to say or ask anything to them. Only you prepare for *"Vidaa"*...think, as if nothing has happened."

Now he could not control himself—"Did really nothing happen?"

"Shuklaji, so many things have happened!"

"OK agreed.... Shuklaji lovingly patted his shoulders..." "But now, when they themselves are ready to do *"Vidaa"* ceremony, then...."

He again laughed.... "You are showing us the acrobatics in the circus, Shuklaji. Is it a game of children or what?"

"Yes, consider a game played out by the God.... Listen, very early in the morning, groom's elder maternal uncle reached. His train was delayed for 15 hours. Very annoyed, he reached my home—since he was my schoolmate. In addition to the disappointment of missing the wedding, this matter of *"Vidaa"* was told to him. He was purple with anger. He went immediately to the lodging place of *"Baraat"*, (not even bothering to finish his cup of tea), while saying, *"Vidaa"* will take place today only and now only! The groom's father respects this man like elder brother. His every wish is command for him;... Now come on, go inside.... Tell them to hurry—I take all the responsibility!"

People standing nearby converged. The lost sheen on the faces returned again. As if they had received the news of the lost treasure being found again! Everyone was saying, "Those people have agreed...they have consented! The problem has been solved." He went inside the house—mechanically.

Ooff! he saw his daughter facing him. He stood there stunned...for few moments! He hesitated before saying anything, and then said, "I came only to say that those people are coming, my child! for... "*Vidaai*"."

"Daughter in bridal dress and make-up looked straight into the sad and worried eyes of the father, as if to ask "*Vidaa*" but how come?"

"Their very close relative has arrived. Just now. He is highly respected by these people. Hence, it is out of question that they will disobey his views. They have sent the message, on their own—Shukla Uncleji was saying—

The daughter heard him very carefully. Then, with same attention, she fixed her sad eyes at the father.

"And you? What do you say?"

This was unexpected. The father was shocked—"I? yes.... I too, my child—came here, just to say that...."

His head had bowed, while finishing the sentence.... Daughter noticed that and said in a very calm and soft tone—in an unwavering manner—"Not like this, I want to hear the directive from my father with his head held high and looking at me directly." "I am scared whether I will lose my father in the bargain of receiving some things.... Assure me, please, that I am not losing!.... See, one thing I want to tell you very clearly, I am ready to tolerate any losses, but I do not want to lose my father, who has been with me for so many years...not at any cost, not on any condition...on the contrary, your daughter will even put everything she owns, at stake, to retain her father safe with her...please understand!"

"My child there is nothing as what you are thinking...you will...with all honour...."

Daughter's voice was soft and friendly, as before—"It is not matter of honour or insult—Do you think we are not used to tolerate insults?... Tell me only one thing... are you happy and fully satisfied?"

"Yes, I am...otherwise it. will be very sad that I am the host of this *"Yajna"* and... *"Poornahuti"* (Final offering) will have to be given by you.... Now you will be happy, your joys will be yours...."

Daughter softly interjected, "You have forgotten—you only have taught us so many times...that happiness and sorrow are the states of mind...we cannot be happy or sad, immediately, as if at the pushing of an electric switch. Isn't it.... Then, similarly, please understand, I also will not be able to place myself in an honourable position so fast! Only by pressing some switch, others will not be able to make me happy, that feeling of happiness has to be felt by me, within myself; isn't it? I too should feel this happiness, isn't it?"

"Then, then what?" the scared father was not able to understand at all what the daughter was telling him...

Suddenly, the daughter became motherly and said—"Shall I tell? Tell Shukla Uncle to go and tell those people... Pardon us for our failings and mistakes...they need not hurry at all—they should consider themselves free from any compulsions. Undoubtedly, we will wait for them as long as they want and also that there is no rancour in our hearts...."

□

7

The Magic Spell

As she heard the taxi's horn, she peeped down with excitement. Yes, that was her daughter there. She felt like jumping down and embracing her daughter.

'Easy, Madam, easy!', she advised herself to restrain. She tucked up her *pallu* and ran down the stairs in a flurry.

The daughter was coming out of the taxi with her five-month-old girl, wrapped in a soft, pink sleeping bag and cuddled in her slender arms.

The mother rushed to take the baby in her arms like a coveted toy.

'Look, be careful,' the daughter smiled with infatuation and embraced her mother.

The luggage was off-loaded from the taxi and taken upstairs one by one. Bags—big and small, bottles of milk and water, box of medicines, towels, mattresses, cushions, tins of milk, powder, etc.

'Your *Maa* has already collected your dowry,' she said to the baby and fondly kissed her again. She then offered to help the daughter, who was carrying a number of bags.

'No please, you only take care of her,' the daughter said with a smile and climbed up the stairs.

The room was full of luggage, due to which it looked smaller. Several bags lay scattered on the floor.

The daughter gave a look to the walls and commented, 'It seems, after I left, you all completely forgot about getting the house whitewashed. Even earlier it was only by my pestering that you got the work done.'

'What? We just got it done now during your wedding.'

'Now?,' the daughter laughed—"It has been seven years since my wedding."

'Seven years!!', that meant she hadn't seen her daughter for five-and-a-half years.

Her eyes were swimming with the revelation—was she really seeing her daughter now or was this an illusion....

The daughter's attention was on the baby. She opened the stand for a swing. 'Give, I'll put her in this.'

'Why so?.. She will stay on my lap,' she said with adoration.

'Staying in the lap will wake her midway through her nap...she will sleep easy in the swing. It's her habit.'

'So what?'

'So? If her sleep is left incomplete, she will bring the whole house down with her tantrums. How will I work then?'

'What work do you have to do?... Anyways, come and have something sweet.'

'I am coming. Just let me change her diaper and sort my stuff out.'

The mother, understandingly, said, 'You have kept everything in a hurry, you will see all of that, what all you forgot, what all you will need for her, you cannot say, can you?'

Whatever maybe she said, the daughter's intelligence had to be praised. 'But first you must eat something. I have been waiting since morning for you to arrive so that we both may sit together and have tea.'

'What? You haven't had your tea yet? Oh, *Mummy*, you are such a....' She looked at her wrist watch.

The mother felt delighted, 'Then what? It's after so many years that we'll be having tea together.'

The daughter was changing the baby's napkin, 'By what time does *Papa* come home?'

'Never before it gets dark.'

'Look, the tea is boiling.'

'I know nothing where you keep the cups and the saucers.' The daughter expressed her desire to help.

"That's good in a way, otherwise a few would have been broken by now." About the daughter, it was known in the family that she moved like a hurricane, causing the end of glassware and crockery, whatever she passed by.

'Come, sit here. *Paranthas* are ready. Shall I give you some chilly pickled in lime juice?'

'Leave it. It may harm her.'

'I am happy you do have that much sense. Now you give her to and have your tea in peace.'

"No, *Maa*. As it is, she is about to wake up. If we change the lap now, she will wake up sooner." As she spoke, she cuddled the baby with deep affection.

Rapt in ecstasy, the mother poured tea and stirred sugar in the cups. She took the first sip of tea with her daughter—sated, satisfied and her heart and soul brimming with an extrasensory pleasure. The two ends of the long period of separation were as if joined by a cord of silk. A bridge made of silk threads. Where should the passage over this bridge start? At the time when the daughter whined in the agony of unbearable suffering after the delivery on a hospital bed in an alien, far off the city.... After deadly dangers and complications when a baby-girl was somehow born, then in spite of all precautions, pus formed in the stitches. Day by day, her body turned pale due to a heavy loss of blood.... The mother kept on hearing all this from others. As it would happen, during that very period her father was hospitalized too. He was in the emergency ward for an appendicitis operation. At that time, there was always that fear in her mind and whenever the phone rang, she was filled with apprehension. What would she get to hear? Living far from each other, that time was spent mostly supported by faith in prayers. Days and months seemed like aeons. Yes.... Where to start?

At that moment, the baby woke up suddenly and began to cry. It appeared that she had roused having a dream in her sleep.

'Look, there goes, the sire. Now I have to report immediately in her service. Thank God, I could at least have some tea.' The daughter at once stood up to make the baby quiet.

'Oh dear, let me hold her,' I say. 'You finish your tea first,' the mother's voice had a trace of anguish in it.

The daughter clarifies in an affectionate manner, 'No, she could be hungry. You know she slept for long in the train. She couldn't take the feed properly.'

'But you should at least finish your *parantha*,' the mother was upset.

'Alright, I'll roll the *parantha* and take it along. Is that fine?'

Just then the daughter caught sight of the *parantha* in her mother's plate. 'You should finish your tea and *parantha* peacefully. I don't need anything.... You haven't eaten since morning.' She left the plate.

'Never mind, but do call me in case you need me.' The mother began to swallow bits of *parantha* without relish.

By the time breakfast got over, it was noon. She quickly winded up and swept the table. She then washed the teacups and took out the vegetables from the fridge but all this while her attention was fixed only on the daughter's voice in anticipation of a call. Though there was none.

Finally, she slowed the burner under the boiling rice and hurried towards the room. It could be that she did not hear the call. The daughter had her back to the door. The mother walked in softly up to her and found that while she lay to feed the baby, she had dozed herself. The mother stood watching this for a while.

For a moment, she thought she should shake her and wake her up. Although she had dozed off, even the daughter must want to talk and share so many matters. But only if she got a chance. Ever since she arrived, she had been busy attending to the baby, she retreated stealthily to let the daughter sleep. She went to the kitchen, strained the boiled rice. The daughter liked rice rather dry. She cut and cooked the vegetables. Added seasoning to the *daal*. The routine chores got over one by one, only flour for making *chapattis* remained to be kneaded.

Suddenly, the daughter woke up. She felt embarrassed and came up to the kitchen. 'Don't know how I got asleep.... Why didn't you wake me up? You should have.'

The mother felt exhilarated. 'Why should I?... It's good you have slept at this time. We shall chat at length in the afternoon. Even I'll feel relieved only after that.'

'In fact, the baby had kept me awake the whole night in the train.'

'Even you used to do the same. Now you understand? No?'

'Who, me? Never. You yourself say that I was a model baby.'

'But even model babies cry.'

'And model mothers keep awake the whole night.' Both had a laugh.

'Now you tell me what's left to be done. All this time you have been doing it alone.'

'You take up your old job of tasting salt in the gravy.'

'What, mangories! Yummy!'

'But when are you going to eat, tell me? You haven't had a bath yet.'

'That doesn't matter, but I have to make fruit juice for her. It's been delayed due to my sleep.'

'Do it now. You don't have to catch a train anymore.'

The daughter opened the basket of fruit, 'Oh God! All these have gotten crushed.... Mummy, can we get some fresh oranges from somewhere closeby?'

'We do have a couple of shops on the next crossing but... who shall go?'

'That Parvati of yours.'

'She? She is a big shirker. She comes like the wind and shoots back like an arrow. Her staying for even a minute extra is out of the question.'

'Is it?' The daughter paused to think. "Then I shall go myself...but what if she wakes up in the meantime?.... The place, the faces, everything is strange to her. You won't be able to manage her."

Suspense prevailed for a while. 'Wait. I shall go and get it.'

The daughter knew that her mother had never before gone on such errands. That was not fair. 'Why trouble yourself? The sun has become hot and severe too.'

'Then do one thing,' she suggested a way out. 'There are some apples in the fridge. I'll cook some. Fruit is fruit.'

'I do give her apple in the evening. But the juice at this time of the day even yesterday in the train I could not give.'

'In that case, let me go and get oranges,' she said in desperation.

Inspite of some diffidence, the daughter's face brightened.

'Alright then, you better get both, oranges and limes. At times, oranges are sour. In that case, you need not take the trouble again.'

When she returned, the daughter was back in her room. The baby was happily rolling and playing on her lap—eyes sparkling like marbles, soft and puffed cheeks. She caressed the baby's forehead relaxingly and asked the daughter, 'Could you not have a bath?'

'How could I? She didn't allow me to do anything. The princess sat wide awake.' The daughter slapped on the doughy back of the baby with a put-on indignation. The mother had the hot sun of the noon on her mind and her stomach was writhing in hunger.

The daughter said, 'Let me first give her a bath. As it is, she is tired after the journey.'

'But what about eating something?'

'I'll have later.'

The mother at once felt like saying, 'And what about me?' But her modesty prevailed upon her and she could somehow think of some other suitable words.

'Such small kids don't get tired that way. Moreover you have travelled in A.C. It would have mattered only if it were hot and humid. In fact, it's you who is tired. Come, let us both eat some hot stuff quickly.'

She had added the word 'both' with an intention or it came up naturally? She was having contortions in her stomach and perhaps in her mind too. The daughter, however, failed to perceive this as her attention was wholly concentrated on the baby.

The daughter said hesitatingly, 'Let me bathe her or else my mind will be stuck there only. Do we have some warm water?'

'I shall heat some on the gas.' The mother hurried towards the kitchen.

The daughter took out a colourful bathtub from the luggage and then one by one she took out baby items—soap, towel, sponge, cream and then added cold water to that.

The mother poured some hot water into the tub and then added cold water to that. That daughter put some water on her fingers and wrist to feel and make sure it was neither too hot nor too cold. Fondling the baby, she said to the mother, 'Now you will have to help me a little in bathing her.'

'Come on, give her to me and see how I am alone able to bathe her quickly....' She tried to get the baby out of the daughter's arms.

'Oh No, Mummy.' The daughter laughed as if the mother was a novice. 'If you make it so hectic, she will blow such a siren that the whole neighbourhood will collect here. She will throw her limbs in agitation and start crying and send the soap and the shampoo to fly. And, above all, she might become averse to bathing.'

The mother was stunned but she could once more find something suitable to say. 'Oh! Now I understand why you refrain from bathing.'

'Exactly.'

Both had a big laugh again. But while she laughed, the mother felt her stomach like an empty bowl with something scraping it from inside.

The daughter made the baby sit in the tub as if that was a demonstration for the mother. Sitting in the water, the baby clasped the rim of the tub in her soft, rosy palms. She looked around fixedly, expressing fear, joy and wonder at the same time.

The daughter engaged herself with full concentration in cleaning the baby's tiny wrists, fingers and even nails in a gentle manner. In between, she kept on smiling and splashing water on the baby. The mother did what the daughter asked her, passing things to her and keeping them back. After cleaning with soap and sponge, there was to be the pouring of water from the tumbler. The mother quickly followed the instructions like 'little by little', 'intermittently', 'now a little behind the head', 'enough', etc. In order to dismiss her hunger, she pretended to look very happy and even fascinated for one, two-and-a-half, three, four minutes.

And suddenly she felt weary, as if she was badly exhausted. But the feeling of boredom was quickly overcome by the realisation of falling in her eyes. An unknown inner feeling reproached her without any reason. She was in a strange predicament.

At such a rare, ravishing moment, boredom was setting inside her. Glumness and fatigue. Was it just because she was hungry? She got perturbed by this plain disinterest growing inside her. What to do? How to conceal it? How to prove herself innocent, without blame? An allegation against her made by herself. All her efforts to evade it were failing. Suddenly, she changed her stance, as if a fresh statement was made on a stamp paper in the court of law. In a confident, jovial manner, she said, 'This stupid woman is unnecessarily bent upon making the child into a duck. Take her out at once. If by any chance she catches a cold....'

The statement brought joy and tenderness back into their conversation. That was the only way to make the daughter realise the long delay. How else could she do it?

But the daughter was completely absorbed in the antics of her child. She was not affected. 'Oh, *Mummy*, you fellows catch cold by a mere mention of water. Do you know children catch cold due to infections and not due to...?'

At that moment, the mother's patience gave in, 'Well, first take her out of the water. You may show off your wisdom then.'

Thank God, for the daughter did feel disconcerted but she could not catch the uneasiness and irritability hidden in the mother's words.

Lost in her own thoughts, the daughter took the baby out and wrapped her in a soft towel to rub her dry.

'Now we will get some relief only after she takes some juice and goes to sleep.' The daughter said realising the mother's problem. Filled with motherly warmth, she kissed the baby again.

After reaching a climax, the mother's appetite had subsided. The empty bowl of her stomach had been upturned.... Lifeless and completely tired, she was only guessing how long the baby would take to go to sleep. The daughter, however, had made the juice before. Now followed the baby lotion, powder, frock, napkin, brushing of hair and, of course, the black mark on the forehead with lamp-soot. Next came the bottle of fruit juice. Sip by sip. May be the baby could doze off while sipping the juice. For the mother, it was like a child counting down the last stages of punishment—five...four...three...two...one.

Suddenly, she heard the daughter saying,' Oh, she is not sleeping. God knows what's the matter.'

The mother's face turned pale. She was not left with energy even to pretend. Yet she expressed concern, 'I hope you gave her enough juice.'

'Yes, everyday she starts dozing while having the juice.' The daughter was visibly worried. More than the baby not going to sleep, she was concerned about the reason for it. Things were going wrong even after her following the schedule by hours, minutes and seconds.

It was afternoon and the maid servant could come any time. The kitchen was still unfinished and open. Meals were not over and things lay as they were.

The daughter understood the matter, 'Come, let's eat like this only. I'll keep her with me.'

'Then what about her sleep?' the mother said. She was hiding her agitation.

'Now if she doesn't sleep, is your kitchen going to be open till the evening? Come we'll eat. Let her not sleep if she doesn't.'

Apparently, the daughter had surrendered, accepted defeat.

The mother served the food after warming it. The two of them began eating together. Even as she ate, the daughter looked sad. Suddenly, she muttered, 'I would have felt relieved if she had slept.'

The mother was surprised that the daughter was not the least fretful. Neither for getting tired nor for having been unable to sleep in the journey. Her only regret was that the baby would have been cheerful when she woke up if she had a good sleep.

The mother felt disgusted. Was the daughter completely oblivious of her presence? There was a spark of vexation closely followed by the smoke of her self-assertion that doused the spark.

But now she was helpless. She clearly felt resentment against the daughter and her baby as if they were a different identity, having no relation whatsoever with her being, her presence. The two of them were like drops of oil mingled together, sparkling on the surface of water while she herself was like the dregs at the bottom.

She clearly noticed that the daughter was just nibbling without any relish that she had prepared with such enthusiasm and after taking such pains that had exhausted her. The daughter's mind was only focused in the baby's eyes.

Suddenly, the mother was startled by her own voice. Thankfully, she said it laughingly and with a sweet expression of jest. 'You are bestowing so much love and affection on this little doll...from the time you have arrived here you are occupied with just looking after her. Since morning, till now, you have tired yourself badly. Will this little girl ever realise all this when she grows up? What do you think, will she ever....'

'Let it not be for me but she will at least do it for her daughter...like you....'

The daughter looked at the baby with an overwhelming perception of joy and shouted as if in disbelief, 'Look, she has gone to sleep. Didn't I tell you?' Flushed with a sense of victory, she proceeded to put the baby on the cot.

□

8

Crossing

Even today, the same thing happened. The signal light turned 'red' just as I reached the fourth crossing and my feet was on the brake, muttering irritably all the time...with petulance.

Even the few seconds are burdensome at such a time.

I have to take a left turn at this place every day on my drive back from work. It is ridiculous, but I never seem to get a green signal here.

And I, too, have this small idiosyncrasy—I hate stopping the car once I have started. And it gets worse towards the end of the day—when I was returning home, dog-tired after a hard day at the office. And today had been especially bad. It had been eight days since Rohini had been advised complete bed rest.

It was a mild stroke. The doctors had been full of the usual homilies and tried to be comforting in their usual manner—"Oh, there is nothing to worry... just need to be slightly careful. Take short walks, try Yoga, reduce salt intake, try to rest more, don't get too excited, slow and careful while sitting down or getting up or walking or avoiding emotional provocation."

'In a way, 85% of my life existence has vanished now. Is it not, Doctor?'

The Doctor had laughed...and Rohini had wept.

Both of us had been getting more depressed steadily.

I had come to the office for the first time today—after seven days of bed rest, leaving her all alone at home. Obviously, I too had been getting impatient. The 'red' signal was jarring more on my nerves. In a bid to try and divert my attention, I turned my head to look around—and saw you standing at the bus stop.

You?

You—who I don't know at all; had never even seen you before today. But right now, at this very moment, as I sought to overcome my irritation, as I sought to pass the time waiting for the light to turn green, my eyes were held by your *Suapankhee* (Teal—a Parrot Green Shade) *'Saree'* and the blouse with the delicate *Bandhani'* print. It was as if the traffic lights had provided you with an opportunity to enter my vision. I had just managed to take in the two thin bangles and the black watch strap when the light suddenly changed—forcing me to move to take the turn and drive away. And was left wondering at how adeptly this word *'Suapankhee'* (Teal) became verdant as a whiff of fresh air across my consciousness.

Of course. I remember now. A long time ago, just once, I heard my mother use this word. There was some function in the house. Amongst all the ladies and girls in the throng, there was this one who had caught my mother's eye. Who knows, maybe even for me. And she went around whispering into the ears of her confidants, 'Did you see? There, that one with the *'Suapankhee'* dress? So what if she is on the darker side—her features are so attractive and vibrant.'

By the time this reached my ears and I tried to get a look, the green *saree* had slipped out of the door. All I had managed to glimpse was the trailing end of the green mantle, but somehow, the image of a beautiful and innocent face had silently crept into some corner of my mind.

But all this was ages ago. It's been, what, ten odd years since even my mother passed away.

...But...come to think of it, wonder where the Green dress is now? Somewhere, certainly grown-up, probably to a Green *saree* now, in some house, some city, possibly even standing at a bus stop....

'*Yeah*, sure—anything else?' I mocked myself—a mature, elderly person to a teenager.

But the young lad was up to it—he had winked back at me naughtily. And the two shared conspiratorial looks, teasing each other...and...slightly abashed also, at the same time.

Home already—the drive seems to have been much shorter today.

Bounded with a light step into the house—and eagerly went up to Rohini. Stood before her with a loving smile—Rohini had liked my smiling at her.

Her stroke had left us in a continuous loop of sadness. We had both suddenly started feeling old. We desperately looked for excuses to laugh, but the laughter just would not come. We anxiously sought to cheer each other up—but found our own confidence ebbing away.

I went close and ran my fingers lovingly through her soft, silvery hair. The togetherness saw the years wash away—it was as if the hair was dark again for both of us. She happily informed me that Neela Malhotra, our neighbour, had dropped by with a pizza—all I had to do was heat it.

That meant that she was already feeling happy that I would get my favourite snack upon my return from the office.

I warmed the Pizza, gave it to her on a plate. Sat her up on the bed, fluffed her pillow and handed the

TV remote to her—so she could watch her favourite programs rather than suffer the usual cricket, wrestling and other juvenile ones that I forced on her.

How is it that we were suddenly closer, happier....

Maybe, that is why, it was easier to leave Rohini and go to the office the next day.

I was a stickler for punctuality.

People could set their watches by when I started my car—colleagues at office as well as neighbours. I had always held that office work should be completed within office hours. Hence, the return from office was always at the same time...

Even if it meant getting the red light at the fourth signal, everyday.

And so it was—today was no exception.

It was a habit to ease my impatience at the signal by looking around—left and right. True to habit, I did. And to my wonder—there you were. Just standing there. The *saree* with finely woven flowers; both hands demurely holding a bag in front—the black strap of the watch.

And perhaps the air whispered softly in my ears—she probably stands here everyday, at this time.

I felt my eyes move up. The graceful neck, with its slim gold chain, supporting the face—utterly oblivious of my stare. Perhaps it was this lack of awareness that gave me more confidence. The velvet *'bindi'*, carefully centered between the two eyebrows. And the solitary jasmine flower tucked away on one side of the neatly collected bun....

The light turned green.

I found myself humming softly as I pressed the accelerator. In my usual off-key voice. But I found my off-key voice not only tuneful but also distinctly lively.

Delved into my right trouser pocket while driving to pull out the folded piece of paper. Rohini had given me her medical prescription—and cautioned me to pick the medicines from the chemist at the crossing as if they were sure to have it in stock.

And so I went to that particular chemist.

Along with the medicines, on an impulse, I also picked up a *'veni'* (a small flower garland) from a street vendor sitting next to the chemist. Even as I began to contemplate Rohini's reaction to my impulsive purchase, you laughed. Just stood there at the bus stop, pointed to the jasmine flower in your hair—and laughed softly.

You? Laugh?

The mature me joked with the teenager—'Well, that action certainly deserved it.'

And my embarrassed visage seemed to be surrounded by the finely woven flowers interspersed with fresh jasmine blooms.

'Oh, you naughty boy…'—the old man was smiling at the youngster.

And the youngster was smiling at you.

And you at me.

And, suddenly, I was home. Much earlier than usual, it seemed.

Though I had stopped to buy the medicines and the *'veni'* for Rohini.

No annoying crowds, no impatiently waiting at the unchanging traffic lights.

Ran up the stairs in my new-found enthusiasm. Opened the door quickly and shut it smartly.

And found myself face-to-face with Rohini.

A happier, more cheerful Rohini compared to the last few weeks. A childlike delight as soon as she saw the *'veni'*. Not the sad, subdued smile of the recent past but one that was full of life. And I noticed her humming softly as I tied the *'veni'* to her hair. Far more melodious and lively than mine.

The same Rohini who had bobbed in a state of helplessness and despair since the 'stroke' had been confirmed.

There was the slender hope she had hung on to as we waited for the test reports to come in. The hope that the doctors were wrong. That the test reports would point to a gastric or some such mild problem. Ever since the reports had confirmed the stroke, she had been in a shell-shocked condition—neither able to laugh freely nor weep her heart out. Just quiet, somber, despondent always.

My cheerful return from office, lively and enthusiastic demeanour, and my happiness—all had perhaps given her some much-needed comfort.

And this became an everyday routine....

The sudden braking at the 'red' signal. Glimpsing you for a few seconds, standing there at the bus stop on the left, the same pose everyday, and moving away when the light changed. And thinking—was the shade of your *saree* a pistachio green today? Delicately balanced between the green and yellow? Or did the lilac shaded saree of yesterday suit you better?

And I suddenly tried to remember—what colour was Rohini's *saree* yesterday. I desperately racked my brains but could not recollect. Nor the shade the day before—or the day before that.... I was beginning to panic....

Glanced around furtively. I hoped no one was watching my nervousness and abashment.

Before this, whatever I possessed belonged to me or was shared with Rohini. Now even when Rohini is absent, I cannot be alone. God alone knows how you enter into the picture. Do you have a secret tunnel into it? But that tunnel comes only up till the bus stop—and vanishes immediately after that.

It is because your place is fixed. You will only have to go and stand up at the bus stop at the fourth crossing, till the signal turns Red, on my reaching there.

Whatever may be my mood, irritated or tired, while leaving the office, by the time I reach the signal, It seems my soul starts searching for you. Trying to guess which *'saree'* you must have worn today. By this time, I have become familiar, not only with all *'sarees'* you wear, but also even the two pairs of *'chappals'* and *'sandals'*. You have only one wristwatch with black strap.

Children? How many and how old? Obviously, must be married. And the husband must be...what would your husband be like, what does he do? So many disconnected, crude queries. Uneasy thoughts. A child-like curiosity.

And suddenly, at times, the curious child grows up and, as if he is a young lad, scolds himself—'Clear off *yaar*'! What is this crude and irrelevant plethora of questions and counter-questions you have collected!

'How are you connected with all this?'

'It may be acceptable to admit somebody in to your existence, but why this meaningless intrusion in her unknown life? It will be better if you control your emotions.'

'OK. Brother, done.'

Really, it was neither an intrusion nor a bad intention. My emotions were also absolutely controlled. Where was the need to tell me to "Behave yourself"?

Next day, I met Mr. Damle from the Packing Department while leaving the office. I stopped the car and gave him a lift when he waved at me. He had missed his bus.

Damle, the chatter box that he is, was gossiping away—the inside stories about all the Departments and the Union. Just then we reached the fourth crossing and the signal turned red.

Excitedly, I turned my head. Carefully—lest Damle notices anything. I must admit thinking—why should the others have any idea about this strange secret? Wholly unnecessary, it will not serve any purpose.

But surprise! Damle was waving his hand, definitely and if my guess was correct, he was waving at you only. Proof? You also had waved back politely.

It was the first time that I had seen you smiling at somebody, who was familiar to you....

Today you were actually smiling. I was stunned. Miles away from your smile, getting entangled in a strange mystery. How does Damle know her? Who can she be? His friend? Relative? Some colleague from a previous job? A small query would have been sufficient and Damle would, on his own, have told me all your background details.

Yes, that is why nothing needs to be asked... As if I did not want to come out of the rainbow like net I had woven for all these days....

Stronger the curiosity, even stronger the refusal—"Nothing will be asked."

Everything will remain as it is. Just as it is. Encapsulated in all mysterious layers. At it's appointed place. As it had been till now.

And should my eagerness and curiosity win over my resolve—well Damle was always there! Let this enchanted mystery remain as it is. Just as it is....

The car was moving on the road.

I was flying in the air.

The next day, while turning at the crossing, I wondered at this fantasy—what if you mistake me for Damle and wave your hand at me? What then?

How strange is the world of dreams, fantasies and conjectures! Idiot that I was, I had forgotten that you will wave your hand only when Damle will raise his hand from the car.

What if I raise my hand.... Oh you fool, how can I wave my hand?

The child in me clapped his hands and laughed—the old man was embarrassed.

I think it was a Friday.

Wow—such a pleasant surprise at the red signal. The hair tied at back in a neat bun and a ceremonial special *'saree';* with *'zari'* brocade, with new ornaments at the neck and ear. Surely there was a 'welcome function' or a 'send-off' party for somebody at the office.

My experience, from all these years of working in an office, tells me that lady colleagues, take out their *'zari'* brocaded *'sarees'* only on such occasions.

Whatever it is, you were looking very different and beautiful also in this changed attire and style.... A thought passed in my mind, today, I will tell Rohini to style her hair as a bun.

At that moment, that naughty child teased me by saying, "Shall I laugh?" and then immediately the signal turned green.

The days went by....

Rohini was recovering from the horror-filled nightmare of the stroke.

Her tinkling smile was slowly returning, and carrying me along with her. Rohini had understood that she needed to make the most of what alternatives were now before her in life. There was nothing to be gained out of a constant self-pity.

I was more than happy to co-operate with her with all my enthusiasm, In a way, the monotony, which had been trying to enter our lives even before Rohini suffered the stroke, was now going away and the life seemed renewed. Like old pots and pans glowing with a new shine after polishing. The pots clashed less often with each other—would sound in harmony else remain in their places neatly.

Rohini had again taken up her old preference of using colourful *'bindis'* and, after a long time, I had again started to try and choose ties while dressing for the office.

Today, this Polka Dot Tie; similar to the *'Bindi'* with your light-blue dress. Anyway, there is this lunch at the Sapphire today, with the American Delegation.

The meeting was good. As was the lunch that followed. I was certainly tired after talking and listening continuously.

Even then, by the time I left office, it was my usual time.

Slowed the car, after speeding it up. Adjusted the tie knot properly with one hand on the steering. I felt better now. Scanned my face in the rear-view mirror. It was all right.

As if I was going to meet some old, close friend...

One, two, three—fourth signal came. Even the signal turned red. Turned my head. Why not to try to show off myself also!

After a momentary bout of indecision, I turned my head—and stared. I could not believe it. You were not there at all. Oh, how can it be! I tried to look more carefully...a little ahead, at the back, but to no avail. You will be seen only when you are there.

The signal had turned green.

Moved on. Reached home.

Rohini looked worried, on seeing me dejected, "You are tired—you take on too much stress."

She placed my socks and shoes in the rack. Brought my slippers. And foam-filled cups of hot coffee, within minutes. Every effort to cheer me back from my feeling of dejection and tiredness.

But I remained entangled, engrossed in my thoughts. I felt drained and angry with myself and felt pity towards Rohini. I patted her shoulders and said, "I have become old, haven't I? These little mood swings will happen some time or the other. She looked detached and dejected, as if we, who were young moments ago, had suddenly reached old age."

Rohini kept hovering around me all the time. Less to know the reason for my sadness and more to get me out of it.

When I tried to stop her, she said, "How much did you look after me during my illness, how much confidence you gave me! It was possible for me to come back to normal due to the strength you gave me. Had you become sad and dejected yourself, I would perhaps have never been able to get out of my depression. All the credit for my recovery goes to you."

Involuntarily I had muttered, with a sad smile, "No, it goes to you."

The next day, and the day after, and after, and after...you were not there, not there at the bus stop.... Not even a sign.

It was as if you had never existed.

I now had started doubting myself.

My other problem was looking Rohini in the eyes—Perhaps scared that my guilt would be caught out. On my return from the office, Rohini used to look at me with hopeful eyes—as if she had been praying for me throughout the whole day.

On the fifth day, unknowingly or perhaps knowingly, I fixed a meeting with Damle during the last hours of the office. Requested him to help me pick up some saplings from the nursery now that the rains were here...after all, he is the plant specialist....

He was more than happy to accompany me. Throughout the journey, he kept on lecturing on the species and subspecies of indoor and outdoor plants. Even while I was listening to the torrent of his speech, my attention was somewhere else.

As soon as we stopped at the signal, I blurted out—"How come you did not wave today?"

"Where? To whom? Oh, her...she was a colleague...in Jack-Anderson...moved to the Head

Office last week on transfer from the Branch Office. Her farewell was last Friday itself. She told me so."

The show had ended! As if the curtain came down and went up again slowly—and all the characters of the play had come on the stage for a curtain call, bowed and gone back....

One by one, all the layers of the mystery had been uncovered, the game of suspense and entertainment had ended....

The stage was empty now...the audience satisfied.

No lingering thrill of suspense, curiosity or eagerness, nor turmoil, nor any feelings of hope, disappointment or sadness.

Within moments, it felt as if the play had ended a long time ago, and there remained only a faint memory.

Everything had settled—flat and levelled.

But I will not let it end in a demoralised manner. This entire episode.

But why? Where was the need for me to do anything?

I climbed the steps and pressed the doorbell, carrying with me a motley collection of saplings and bulbs...

Was the press of my finger on the bell different from the other days?

Was it like in the earlier days—full of hope and enthusiasm?

Perhaps Yes....

That is why, probably, Rohini opened the door in an impatient haste to regain something which she had lost—and beamed with happiness when she saw my face. As if we had met after getting separated in a crowd, as we stood, clasping each other's hands.

And that entire evening, like enthusiastic children, we planted, one after the other, the saplings in the various pots, filled with soft, powdery earth.

□

9

GRANDPA AND MONKEYS

Grandpa is visiting us again.

Again, he is missing my children very badly.

On hearing this, I banged my fist on my head, with annoyance. Indeed, this issue really deserved the banging of head. He had come to us in the summer holidays just a while back, not even a year had passed since. He had stayed for not one or two months—but a full six months! That too, would he depart on his own will and wish? I suggested craftily and smartly that he should go back to our village and look after our ancestral land and property. Otherwise if it is neglected and left uncared for a longer period like this, the farmers who are tending it, would disown us and take over the farm and property. A loss of thousands of rupees – for no reason and due to our negligence. Hence, we should look after and keep watch on our property periodically.

After all this coaxing, he understood finally. The luggage and bedding was packed and made ready. Even then, while leaving, even after sitting in the car, he kept on turning back and looking back at the children he was parting from. Lalit had to curtly remark, "Children have gone in the house, now sit back properly."

Then also, wiping his tearful eyes with the napkin, he kept on repeating, "Now I am so old – like a ripe fruit, will fall down any time – don't know whether I will be able to see the children again in this life or not. Also, now it is not possible to travel alone, on my own. My body has become weak. That daughter-in-law of mine is wise, who has advised me to look after our house and farm at the village. She keeps track of all the things and looks after everything. May God keep her sharp and wise like this only...the only problem is being away from you all...." "Now I will not be able to see you all again."

"Oh Yes! You will see and meet us again. Don't say such things!"

Controlling his craving for a cigarette, Lalit had carefully made a light, meaningless remark and imagined that he has taken a deep puff of cigarette and had flicked off the cigarette ash.

On returning home, Lalit had burst into laughter, while narrating all this. "Do you know what was I thinking at that time? I was thinking that at this emotional outburst, like a true loving son, had I said lovingly that 'If you do not feel like going, then do not go.... Forget the hassles and labour to be undertaken for a piece of land.... Let us return home, back to the children', what have been your condition on seeing him back home... Ha... Ha... Ha..." But instead of that, like true, wife-loving and devoted husband, I had said, "Oh, Oh, you will certainly come back."

While saying this, Lalit definitely must have prayed God for the forgiveness – 'Oh God! please forgive me, for even after knowing everything, my giving him false hope, to make him feel better... otherwise I know it fully well that, after this time, his worn-out body will not now return to our home.'

But, no Sir! With all his tired limbs collected together, Grandpa is coming back! It is not even a fortnight that we have arrived in this new town and Grandpa is pining for meeting the children. He is feeling as if the last one and a half years are more than many aeons. He keeps on seeing children's faces, all the time! (Must ask him, then where is the need to come here! If he keeps thinking about the children and their faces all the time, that means he is not separated from them). Anyway, now we must get up and prepare for the arrival of Grandpa.

No idea, why these old people keep their hearts overstocked with love and affection. Always ready to shower it. As if their hearts have become like a marshy land due to their love and affection – they make our life really difficult!

Lalit objects, "What? Your life becomes difficult? This is too much, my dear. All throughout the day he sits, with his head lowered – in one or the other corner of the house. If you offer him tea, he will drink it. If you serve him food, he will eat it. He will eat whatever is given. He will eat whenever it is offered. He washes his own clothes, may be not very clean, and spreads them out for drying...."

"No doubt, but where?" I got a chance to retort angrily. "Right in the front corridor, strung across like festoons – towel, napkins, undergarments and *dhoti.* Then who brings back those inside and spreads on the clothes-line? On top of it, who gets the oily pillow cover scrubbed over and over again – which becomes sticky from the cupful of sesame oil (brought from village oil mill) applied by him to his head?.... Oh, the whole room stinks of sesame oil and mustard oil, as if the oil crusher has been set up in the room itself."

Lalit likes to make me angry, "But then, does he not help you with some of your work? Twice a day he dresses up, takes his umbrella and drops and fetches back Shanu and Shaunak to and from the school. Whether it is under a hot sun or in the rains, whether he is feeling low or feverish...did he not dig up the backyard and plant and produce vegetables like tomato, spinach, lady fingers, etc.? And if not anything, we have saved thousands of rupees in so many months, by not purchasing these things...."

"Hmmm..." I sulked, out of that, the shop keeper must have usurped hundreds of rupees by making false calculations or large amount of money must have fallen out of pockets of Grandpa...had it not been for these things, why was I sending him with the maid-servant, to buy the provisions from the store? I thought the maid-servant's scam of pilfering the grains, by fistfuls, at the shop itself, will be kept in check by Grandpa...but look what happened? The maid, instead, came back laughing, as if to mock me. Came to know that after the purchasing of provisions, she asks Grandpa – "Grandpa, shall I take two fistfuls of sugar and put it in my skirt pocket, for my children?" And Grandpa will reply, "Why two fistfuls, take four – why do you ask? It does not matter...."

But Lalit will not stop teasing me. He was firm in his stance—"You are really a very ungrateful woman. But it is not your fault. Wives win any argument and have been winning for hundreds of years. Just by listening to wife's arguments, the poor man's brain becomes numb. He has no energy left to talk.... In any case, get this in your mind that there is no way by which his arrival here can be stopped...."

"That was true. I was sad and disappointed. But the smart horses of my mind started running in various directions, came to the conclusion that it's OK. Since now he is indeed visiting us, for my satisfaction, if not for anything else, Grandpa should be useful for some purpose. In exchange of his stay here and keeping him here, any type of relief or concession.... But our gardener too comes regularly every alternate day, for an hour or so. It is better if we do not disturb his schedule. Children also are going to Queen Mary's Convent by *rickshaw*. After Lalit's promotion, we have taken them out of Hindi school."

To leave them or to bring them back from school, no Grandpa is necessary. I felt a need for some errand boy or watchman-type person to do the odd jobs, who will rush out and smartly salute Lalit and open the gate, when Lalit comes back in the evening, by car. He will also serve snacks and tea to the visitors. He will rush to the shopping market in the square to bring some soda or beer – High status of the officers rests on such things only! But Grandpa was not fit and useful even for these things...still I have to think of some remedy on this, and will have to make useful for something or the other...this "Useless" Grandpa....

I was busy thinking on the same problem, even my afternoon siesta was delayed and still I kept on thinking for something or the other... for some trick for making Grandpa useful... it was very difficult to go to sleep.

Must have been half an hour or so, then I suddenly heard *Dhoom-Dhadam, Dhood-Dhood* and mad shouting on our roof... woke up to see what all this was when I saw Lalit was already at the window. I went and looked at the spectacle. I was stunned and shocked... All around our home, about 20-25 small and big monkeys were jumping and giving loud cries. We were surrounded by them....

There is a small street at one side of our house and an empty plot of land at the other side. Only after our many shouts of help, Mrs. Gupta, the wife of tin plater, who lived at the backside of our house, said very calmly, "You have recently come here to stay, Is not it...monkeys do always come here...in similar groups of about 20 or 25 sometimes for two to four weeks or sometimes only for a few days.... There is no way to predict their schedule of stay. Monkeys are not even scared of children...the best thing is to close the door of the house, then what damage will they do?... But anyway they are monkeys, they are bound to destroy trees, leaves, gardens, saplings and potted plants. For this reason only, we have not maintained any plants or garden, etc. But I see, you have kept a gardener too, stop his services from tomorrow. Its not worth the bother."

'Oh! at the behest of wife of tinplater? our gardener does not cost us, his services paid for by the government, free of cost to, as a perk to Lalit. Why should we forsake his services? It will be so insulting! He will definitely come every alternate morning and will plant saplings and will nurture the garden. But who will get rid of this marauding gang of monkeys, which will come intermittently?'

Suddenly, there was a lightning struck in the form of an idea in my mind.... Oh Yes.... Grandpa....

And my heart, which was heavy, as if it was loaded with tonnes of weight, was feeling a little lighter.

The load became still lighter, when, in the next week, the monkeys attacked us thrice. After every few days, suddenly the house would be surrounded by the monkeys in the vacant plot, at the side of our house, a few of them would be fighting and screaming at each other. They would snap and break the branches of the guava tree, Biting off and uprooting plants of tomato and brinjal.

Me, alone, and young Shanu and Shaunak. The monkeys ground their teeth in a wild manner, when once we wielded a stick and shook it at them from the safety of a window. Their wild reaction sent a shiver down our spine. We could neither control our fear nor our anger. I was watching from my closed house, through each window and ventilator, one after another, the destruction of my newly planted saplings and garden; as if I was in a cage, wild, like the monkeys themselves! Many times, the door of the house could not be opened for hours together due to attack by wild monkeys...at that time, I felt light-hearted at the thought of coming of Grandpa.

At last, Grandpa arrived. (He had to come anyway). Immediately, after he came, Shanu and Shaunak showed him the stick.

"Do you know what is this? This is a stick mother has kept for you...."

"Yes...." Grandpa started to examine it, while nodding his head happily, "I will use it as a walking stick, while I go for my walk... Sometimes dogs chase you...."

"Oh no," they said scornfully. "No, it is not to be used for beating dogs. It is to chase away the monkeys...with this, you will chase away the monkeys."

"Monkeys? Where are the monkeys?" Grandpa asked with curiosity.

"They do come, sometimes too many of them." Then both of us and Mummy are very much scared....

...But it is fun also when they do somersaults and when they give shrill cries while fighting with each other in the backyard. You will also enjoy if you see these things, isn't it Shanu!

"But take care and look after your spectacles," advised Shanu.

"OK, OK...." he listens to children's prattle with great interest. Then he opens his suitcase with the same interest and takes out a plastic-covered photograph of *Hanumanji* (Monkey God) and one stuffed elephant, made of black cloth. He hands over the elephant to them, with the air of, 'look, what I have brought for you.'

Children carelessly toss away these two gifts and say, "What will we do with this? Did you not have a photograph of Amitabh Bachchan instead?"

Grandpa starts to preach the kids, enthusiastically about greatness of *Hanumanji.*

Shaunak says disdainfully, "We know, all these monkeys come only from the yard of *Hanumanji* temple, near the *peepal* tree. This entire nuisance is due to the same *Hanumanji.*"

Grandpa is contented by the chatter, carefully takes out few bags of seeds of various vegetables. On seeing this, children again start squealing, "keep it back, back in the suitcase! There will be no sowing of any kind. Do you not know? *Papa* has been promoted in his job. Now a gardener comes here for that. You only have to chase away the monkeys and nothing else, do you understand?"

Definitely he did not understand, on the third day itself, he slipped away from our watchful eyes and approached the gardener. After exchanges of salutations and greetings, they got to know each other. So much so that now Grandpa is mending the garden by using various gardening implements like pick axe, shovel, etc. and the gardener is sitting and smoking *bidi*, under the shade of the black currant tree. I banged my head with fist, in desperation and thought that if the gardener's service were not free of cost, I would have immediately dismissed him and made a profit of few hundred rupees.

In the evening, I shouted angrily on any pretext. I appealed to Grandpa's age-old wisdom and his son's status of senior officer and insisted that his behaviour should be sensible and appropriate....

While listening to the above, Grandpa was shaking his head with such an obedient gesture, as if I am scolding some absolutely useless and lowest level person and he himself pities the ignorance of that man, by agreeing with what I was saying.

He was very impatient throughout the next day. Kept on asking children, "The gardener has not come today?"

Children also got annoyed, "Did we not tell you that the gardener comes every alternate day? He will not come today, will be here tomorrow."

Third day, when the gardener came, Grandpa was sleeping, with his head covered by a napkin. Children were busy with their homework. I was relieved. But after half-an-hour only, children came running and shouting, "*Mummy!* Grandpa has cut himself in hand, while using tree trimming scissors, blood is gushing out...."

I ran to him, only to see him with lowered head, washing the flowing blood under the water tap. On seeing me, he hid his wounded finger in the loose end of *dhoti* and scooted quickly to his room, like a frightened child.

Following him were shouting children, "How are you enjoying it now? Just now you were merrily cutting and snapping the shrubs and trees... When we tried to prevent you, you had said, Oh nothing will happen.... Now what? What will you say now...."

He was ashamed but with a smile, he pressed his injured finger, with an end of his *dhoti* and kept on telling Shaunak to take out the tablet of Alum from his shaving kit...its application would stop the flow of blood.

Now, I had to do something. Giving in to the situation, I dressed up the wound with an ointment and bandage...but I was livid with anger....

"At last, on the fourth day, the monkeys arrived. I was relieved. The children were present at home, at that time." As soon as they saw the monkeys, they shouted, "Monkeys have come, Monkeys are here, Grandpa! Come on, Take the stick and chase out the monkeys...."

Grandpa really wielded the stick, like an obedient child and went out in the outside corridor...as if it was some new game of children. But he was stunned and horrified to see the scene, all around. On each arch of the parapet, one monkey or the other were sitting with their many offspring. They were busy in scratching each other's backs, hitting each other, pulling each other's tail or were biting off flowers, leaves from tree branches.... The entry of Grandpa with children was great interference in their above activities and personal life. On seeing two children and one old man, that too with a stick, the monkeys gnashed their teeth, from wherever they were sitting and adopted a scary mask-like monkey face.

Grandpa got scared and his stick was lowered automatically and the screaming children ran back in the room. Horror and enjoyment at once and together... Immediately on coming into the room, they pushed Grandpa out and shouted:

"Chase them off Grandpa, chase them out, do not get scared; they will never bite you. They only scare off children and ladies. They are scared of men...will not bite you...."

Grandpa again went out. He fearfully rattled his stick, but the monkeys sat at their places, without taking notice of his stick. This enthused the children to a large extent, because earlier I used to get scared and run back in the house and shut off all doors and windows the moment I heard of monkeys' arrival! My heart used to beat faster, just by seeing children at the windows, watching the monkeys. But today, the children were pacified because of the presence of Grandpa. Children were jumping, shouting and mocking the monkeys. After some time, as if the monkeys were bored, all of them shifted to another area and *Shanu-Shounak* were screaming their heads off, "Monkeys have run away, all of them have run away."

My satisfaction and happiness were more for finding the usefulness of Grandpa, rather than avoiding the destruction of flowers and garden. I was encouraged by this success and then tried to speed up the horse—that was my brain—like this, some more uses and utility of Grandpa should be found out.

But within a week, I discovered something and all my wishes and expectations were washed out. What happened was, on the fifth day, the monkeys came again. Not one or two but a total gang or a complete clan arrived. They were in the outer corridor, in the backyard, on the roof, on the staircase, on the water tank, on the roof, on the TV antenna, on clothes-line and in every possible place. Saplings and plants in the garden were crushed due to their jumping around and biting them off. I was livid with rage, "Oh Grandpa, you have not yet chased off these monkeys? Like children, you also are enjoying the scene, by watching it through the window? Oh! Chase them off, make them run away, immediately! If all the garden and saplings are destroyed, then what is the point in chasing them off?"

But many times, on my insistence, Grandpa went out slowly with the stick, then he used to get scared on seeing a wild monkey gnashing its teeth at him and, hence, he would come back running into the room. While running into the room, one end of his *dhoti* got caught in a protruding nail on the door and his *dhoti* was torn.... After this, I insisted many times to go out, but he used to shout from inside only. On top of it, the funny part was he tried to fool me by uttering some phrases like 'chased them away', 'they will move away on their own', 'they are not doing any damage, I am watching them', 'as soon as they cause any damage, I will chase them away'.

In week after the above incident, everything became very clear. I had gone out shopping for about 2-3 hours. On return, I found that on the steps at the entrance, 2-3 pots of flowers were toppled and, after entering the house, I saw all my trees, flowers, the garden were scattered and destroyed.

I was seething with anger. On seeing me, I saw Grandpa scooting into the bathroom first and then immediately sit in front of the idol of God, *Shrikrishna,* to say prayers.

Even children, though very young, had sense enough – on seeing Grandpa, they immediately started yelling, "*Aahaa!* Now you are pretending to pray and sit silently, because you are scared of mother. You were not able to chase away the monkeys, that is why you are scared of *Mummy.* We coaxed him very much saying go and chase away the monkeys, the more you get scared the more these monkeys will get bold and scare you further.... Go, at least make an effort...but he did never consent to our request."

"I pursed my lips, gave him a scornful look and went inside the house, boiling with rage and anger."

To say anything about this to Lalit was absolutely of no use. He would either make fun of the whole thing or remain silent. My rage instead was directed towards the children while I was making them do their homework. Actually, they broached the matter, "How badly our garden is damaged. Didn't you say that

Grandpa will keep on chasing the monkeys away, but he himself is so scared of them."

"My rage burst out with full force, if he is so much scared, he should go back to the village and scare away the birds and crows from the farm.... What use he has for us here. As the saying goes...."

I did not utter that saying, by controlling my emotions and did not want children to hear it. But the children certainly communicated the rage filled visage of *Mummy* and her saying something about Grandpa going back to village.... As it is, my direct communication with Grandpa was limited only to asking him to table for tea-breakfast or lunch and dinner. Rest of the communication was through Lalit and children – for example, 'Do not apply so much of oil!' Please rub and clean the shoes properly on the shoe mat, before entering the house...!

He now started to follow these instructions strictly, with much more care than was necessary. He used to rub clean his shoes very thoroughly on the shoe mat, in front of me. Unknowingly, he will spread his towel on the clothes-line and then will remember my instructions, and will remove it immediately. He will tell the children that, "Now I do not apply too much of oil. It smells, you know." And on addition to this, he even started to go to the nearby shop, if Shanu-Shaunak wanted to buy even pencil or eraser. He will immediately take his umbrella to go out and say softly, "OK, I will get it for you... ask *Mummy* if there is any other thing to be purchased.... I will go and get it...." Not only this, but he had even started to do salvage operation to the destroyed plants and garden with all his might and effort, before the gardener came.

But the monkeys arrived again within the next 3-4 days. Again the plants, flowers and garden were damaged. I used to peer through the window, bite my lips and stalk in the room from end-to-end. Grandpa was in a fix! Just to show me, he will try to look out by opening the door ajar. But on looking at monkeys, even at their little gnashing of teeth, he will be stricken with fear and close the door.

On coming face-to-face with me, he will avoid my gaze and turn away to walk silently and sit in some corner of the room, on any pretext. My rage and anger used to get converted to some sort of madness. It was a strange teeth-grinding situation going out of control.

In this atmosphere, I used to get maximum and total satisfaction, when children used to tease Grandpa, a man who is, "scared and fear-stricken".

Actually, my whole plan was becoming a flop. On top of it, even after hiding my impatience and anger towards Grandpa, was clearly understood by him. As it is, even before this, when I was making sweet talk with Grandpa! But now we were strategically opposite each other. He was plotting in his defense and I was minding my defense. Breakfast is served, lunch is kept on the table. Breakfast and lunch are not served to him, but they are put in front of him. He also will eat silently and walk off.

One day, while doing homework, children asked him, "Now you will have to go back to your village, isn't it?"

"Why?"

"Because you are not able to chase off the monkeys...you are scared of them."

Grandpa was stunned and sat silently. He was not able to understand what should he say in his defense? After a few moments, as if he was telling some new thing to the children, he said, "These monkeys are incarnation of *Hanuman*, the Monkey God."

On this, the children started laughing heartily. Grandpa watched them like a fool. He had not expected this. He had thought that children will agree or disagree with his statement...and the matter will be discussed and proceed further, but the children had laughed away and it was like, "Innings being declared closed." Grandpa sat silently like a fool. Then he got up depressed, took the stick, put on sandals and went out, just to wander here and there.

He returned.

He will not sit at one place—will move from this corner to that corner.

Will follow the children, everywhere, as if he was their shadow; now even children started thinking how to avoid him. When they were very young, we used to laugh at their childish, baby talk, but now they are speaking fine English...they get bored and say – 'Is your joke over or not...' and they laugh with uproar. Now children are no more young – reading, writing, sports and all other distractions...then have to complete homework on time. Only while doing homework do the children sit quietly, stay at home.

Yes, Grandpa will come and sit in a corner near the children silently and watch them do homework – glancing around stealthily to see whether I am nearby or not. Then he will try to talk to children on any subject, for example – 'You know, your father is my son, in the same way, you are his sons...he was also a young child and I used to scold him exactly like he scolds you.'

...Then he will think for some time and add—'He was very scared of me' or sometimes—'Just as he brings chocolates and biscuits for you, I also used to bring these sweets for him... I had bought the costliest hat and soldier's dress for him....'

Then one day, after much consideration, he told a thought, in front of children, "If I go back to village, how will I be able to see all of you..." and with an impatient face, waited for the children's reply.

But children did not realise the seriousness of this remark at all. They heard it and said 'Yes' and nodded. They bent their back and went back to their homework.

Grandpa kept on sitting. He suddenly got up and as if he was very busy, put on his sandals, took his umbrella and went out.

At home, I was also busy with urgent chores, was unaware of his departure. Late in the evening, I thought about him.... I was worried that this old man may have slipped and fallen somewhere. At that time, I saw him cleaning his sandals on the shoe mat. Where had he been?

Had gone to the temple. But what were you doing there for all this time? I was accompanying a, "Prayer Singing Troupe", on cymbals and offering them rhythm for their song. The reply came with much pride and satisfaction.

OK fine, you play cymbals or drums, it is none of our concern.

But after a few days, he came back early and, when asked, he maintained silence, as if he did not want to tell. Afterwards, Lalit told me, laughing, that the singing troupe has gone away and the new troupe has their own cymbal player. That is why, he was a little dejected.

So be it, but it is the Temple of *Hanumanji* – a sacred place. He goes and sits there (who knows one day their cymbal player will be absent).

Then one day, the maid-servant informed, "Who Grandpa? He does not spend much time in the temple! I always see him near the vegetable vendor plantation of tomato, brinjal, beyond the bridge. There he chats with them about their methods, fertilizers, produce and general things."

Lalit's anger was justified, but even then he controlled it. He just advised Grandpa curtly in short sentences that he should go up to the temple only. That's all. There was no need to sit here and there, talking to sundry people.

Grandpa agreed to it, without any discussion or argument. As if to say, what you are saying is absolutely right and he will not roam around anymore. Only from house to the temple and from temple to the house, that's all.

Monkeys used to come, as usual, even now, but nobody would say anything to Grandpa. Keeping aside our high status, I, maid-servant and children would start making wild noise by beating empty tin cans and plates from inside only... people moving on the road suddenly got alarmed and then would smile at us and move ahead. We, inside the room, would get very much embarrassed but the monkeys would get tired and defeated by all the noise and would leave one by one.

Then we would relax happily and the children would tease Grandpa by saying, "Did you see! We ourselves chased away the monkeys."

Suddenly, one day, Lalit came home, happy and joyful. Got an order to visit and stay at the site for ten days. The best thing was his Boss had permitted him to take his wife and children along with him. Small place, in a forest and in the valley. Contractor, supervisor will be at our service all the time and will be available at our beck and call. Would earn extra money also. Very good picnic and, the best thing was, we need not search for a watchman, who will charge 15 rupees a day. Grandpa of course, was there for it.

Lalit himself explained—"We all are going away for a few days. Look after the house. Be careful. On hearing this, he seemed to be scared from inside, like a small child—'For how many days will you all be away?, I will go to the village, if you will be gone for a month or so...." But I winked at Lalit—now when there is some work, to look after the house, he is avoiding that. Lalit said, "Oh No...only for a week-but could be delayed for a few days. After all, it is my job, not my personal work. And what is your problem? At the village, you used to cook yourself. Here we will instruct the maidservant to do all the work. She will cook once only in a day, which will be enough for you for the day. But please remain in the house only, throughout the day. Do you understand?

"And if the monkeys come, make noise of tins and plates from inside only," said children, at which Lalit and myself laughed heartily.

While cleaning the utensils and plates, the maid laughed and remarked, "Poor Grandpa, everybody makes fun of him because he is scared of monkeys..."

When we were ready to depart, Grandpa was waiting impatiently. Then he himself tried to console us by saying—as if we are very sad and worried to leave him alone in the house—"Do not worry about me... I am used to stay all alone, for months and years, in the village... cooking the food is no problem now. If there is pain in my joints, I will take the yellow tablet. And will apply turpentine oil to my knees. Rest of the time, I will go and sit in the temple, that's all."

Anyway, he kept on comforting and saying on our behalf to himself, what we should have told him and we started our car and left.

On reaching the site, everything turned topsy-turvy and against our expectations. So much so that we were left to ourselves to do all our work. We had reached full of hope and high in spirits, but all that crumbled. After just two days, Lalit's boss himself landed at the site and the welcome and service we had expected from the junior staff, Lalit had provide the same for his Boss.

In fact, he was the most tense, nervous person, amongst the staff. The reason was that all the responsibility at site for the project was Lalit's. Now throughout the day, for many days, he was running after his Boss with all the files, registers, etc. He had no time even for breakfast or dinner. Whatever free time he had, he used to spend it in the service of the Boss, so that his service record would remain clean and proper.

In spite of his Boss's telling, he would not leave but would be at his beck and call, will come to our tent extremely tired, late at night and would go to sleep. I and children were trapped in the tent – worse than a prison, with no fun or enjoyment. Even the animals in the circus are brought outside in the circus ring for the show. We were scared even to venture out of our tent, walk a few rounds. Children used to be taken out with thousands of warnings and instructions.... If we come face-to-face with the Boss, behave like this, say good morning... That is how our picnic turned out to be. Not only children, but even I was feeling suffocated.

In this atmosphere, I used to pine for our home. Naturally, I was worried also. Apart from the home, I used to think about Grandpa also – Is he alright? Is he sick or what? That will be another hardship when we return. If he had kept any door open, by mistake, that will be another debacle. Monkeys must have damaged everything. Oh my God! How we have been trapped here...and there, Grandpa is also all alone...for so many days, for so many hours, what would he be doing on the monkey gang arrival? How much noise can he make by beating tins and plates? Lalit had prevented him even from going to temple, with the fear that he might drop and lose house-keys somewhere. On observing that nobody is at home, what if thieves enter from the backyard window? Thousands of doubts, millions of possibilities.... "Please sit quietly at home – Have your food regularly and do your worship and prayers of God. Two weeks will pass, just like that...."

I was realising that now. Extreme boredom and suffocating loneliness... sadness. All the work was important, running around the Boss, obsequiousness towards him—in this, Lalit had no time for us, as if he was unaware of our presence there. Sadly, the two weeks turned to four weeks. Oh, when will all this end? This homeless state, suffocation and monotony, when will we be free of all this?

At last, we got the freedom. The site work was completed and we were relieved. We left by car, on the same day. On our way back, I was thinking about Grandpa, how he must have lived alone, for so many days.

The car stopped, gate was opened, I ran madly and climbed the outer corridor's steps. And I was stunned and shocked. Our entire corridor was full of small and big monkeys and Grandpa was sitting on a chair at the door. He was feeding soaked grains by fistfuls to the monkeys. The younger monkeys to express their happiness were doing somersaults in front of Grandpa to please him. They were obviously pampered by Grandpa. And Grandpa was happily watching them.

The maid-servant, standing by the support of the door-frame, was watching all this lovingly and Grandpa was explaining to her proudly—'Monkeys are incarnation of *Hanumanji*, the Monkey God....'

□

10

The Girl with Unshed Tears

The girl has suddenly come and stood in front of me!

Almost everything in the house had been packed. Just a few things now scattered around the house and my writing table—the same table on which I was bent over, running my pen furiously, as if being swept along in a strong current.

The interruption comes almost as a shock, as I bent over the table. Two big eyes, heavily coated with Kaajal, were peering from behind the door—one end of a turquoise blue Dupatta slowly fluttered into view. She hesitated for a moment and stood still, shy, undecided, at the door. Then she came in and stood laughing in front of me.

"Auntie!"

She extended a bouquet of fresh long stemmed Asters, clutched in her hands, towards me.

"This is for you!" Again, the shy helplessness in her lowered eyes.

Accepting the flowers, I see 6-7 fresh Asters, surrounded by green ferns with glitter on them, all tied together with a yellow silk ribbon!

"Oh – Thanks! Thanks a lot...the flowers are really beautiful." Some agitation rattles my entire body – a convulsion across my entire consciousness. Everything is topsy-turvy, unstable. Despite the turmoil, a question manages to sneak its way across to me, secretly and yet cutting across the confusion. "...Her? Suddenly? From where? And more importantly, why?

She turned nervous and timorous as she felt my eyes on her. Probably wondering what to say and how to say it, now that she had come. One could see her heart pounding away."

Then somehow, collecting all her strength and courage –

"How are you...Auntie?"

"I? umm? Well yes, I am absolutely fine," I said, somehow controlling my stammering.

"But wait, I should first arrange these flowers in a vase, shouldn't I! " And I run into the kitchen with the flowers, dodging her gaze and avoiding her eyes. I really needed to control and present myself to her naturally – and to collect my scattered thoughts.

Oof, that sweet, pure look and the tempest within myself! She...why has she come? It is possible that she has come just like that. We are getting transferred after all. So many people come, just to meet, to enquire our well-being and to ask if we need any help. But why has she come? (As if all others have a right to come, but she should not have come at all). Suspicious, apprehensive – questions again start scattering themselves all over. I was mechanically arranging the flowers in a beautiful vase. Maybe I was using the opportunity to arrange myself – to sort my feelings out so I can present myself to her in a more composed manner when I face her back.

"See, how beautiful these flowers look!"

I have arranged the Asters in a vase on the cornice. With the same demure and shy manner, she smiled and nodded her agreement.

"You always arrange flowers beautifully Auntie. Just look at these roses...."

A sense of pride fills me up. Just this morning I had arranged fresh roses – pink, red, cream and bright – right at the centre of the round glass table.

And on the table in the corner – a few sticks of Rajanigandha.

But I don't know why, I found the white Asters to be far more elegant compared to these two. Modest, unpretentious, calm and demure! As if someone is content to remain standing there throughout his life, waiting to be understood.

Do I know the reason for this sad and helpless smile?

No—No, definitely not! As if somebody clamps my mouth shut from behind and I try to sneak away through the back door. But stubbornly, the question follows me everywhere—why am I not able to behave and talk naturally with the girl? Standing in front of her, why can't I ask her even the usual polite questions etiquette and courtesy demand? Instead, she is the one asking me, in the most cultured way—

"Auntie are you leaving...all of you are going from here?"

"Oh! Yes...you understand nothing can be done about it – we have to go."

"When?"

Words full of some strange sadness and defeat, trembling, yet controlled admirably.

"When Auntie?"

A deceptively simple question, but one that starts turning my doubt into a firm belief. I have again become alert, watchful—and cleverly parry the question with an inane response, without any assurance.

"Well, cannot say exactly when, but any time. You can see how everything is scattered here and there."

She remains unaware of my maneuvering. Looks at the things scattered around the house with the same simple and guileless sympathy.

You.... Really must be getting tired, is'nt it! How and what to pack and where. I was thinking that I should have come over and given you some help...."

"No, no—No need...." I immediately cut short the stream of sympathy. "All that is anyway being handled very well by the professional packers, thanks!"

She is intimidated and again goes quiet.

I observe her covertly from the secret door. Does she know that I have some idea of the purpose behind her visit? But is that purpose impudence on her part? Or is it just the manifestation of some deep, hitherto untouched but pure feeling! The helpless pangs of an artless but vulnerable person....

No... No, all this is my imagination. The truth is that this girl has a passing acquaintance with me and my family, that's all! And that she is an expert in "Bridal make-up." That is why I had specifically called her to do my daughter's wedding make–up. She had very joyfully accepted to do it and left no stone unturned to carry out the responsibility to the best of her ability. She started working with my daughter several days in advance, trying out several combinations and seeking my approval. And on the day of the wedding, I was enthralled by her dedication and concentration. To tell you the truth, engrossed as she was in doing the bridal make-up, I found her looking more beautiful than my daughter. One and all had been full of praise for the 'make–up' and now my daughter was at her in-laws, a newly married bride.

"How is Medha, Aunty? I hope she is fine?" she tentatively breaks the silence."

"Yes—Yes...she is well...." The question surprises me—and makes me wonder guiltily why I am unable to reply with even a full sentence. To break my edginess, I hope to get away by responding with a common cliche.

"Medha was here last Sunday; she was asking about you too."

"Oh really." As if she was grateful for my words. There appeared a glimmer of hope in the midst of her sadness, but vanished immediately.

Oh! The image she presented. Like the prelude to a tragic story that did not leave any soul untouched. A sudden thought came to my mind—How I wished I could put this, all this exactly—as it was, into the story I was currently writing. That would have been my most emotional and heart-rending gift to literature – that clear and pure gaze, drooping eye-lashes under the layer of kajal and beneath all that, the dim and flickering glow in the eyes.

The roses, in their delicate bone china vase with gold trimmings, are only too aware of their majestic appearance, the Rajanigandha sticks have a self-conscious modesty, but the Asters, they remain standing gracefully, modest, patiently waiting. A mildest tremor runs across them, like that on the lips of this girl sitting in front of me.

Asters cannot talk. But surely the girl can talk.

Her lips did move, trembled again. But why didn't she say anything?

Maybe words have not been created so far to be able to express what she wants to say. That is why, though she tries to speak now and then, but has to give up and stare helplessly towards the Asters instead.

And the Asters too, all they have been able to convey is that this girl also needs a bed of flowers to nurture her anguish.

Anguish? I am startled back to the reality.

Now where has all this talk of anguish and melancholy arisen from? All we had been talking about was the green fern, yellow ribbons and my creativity. Why leave that beautiful conversational thread and talk of melancholy? Who is this girl to me, after all – just a casual acquaintance? Is it not asking too much to expect me to nurture and handle some unknown melancholy she may be wallowing in? How can I be expected to be aware of any sadness she carries?

Then, as if some invisible hands have throttled my voice and asked me in an ominous tone "Do you really not know about the melancholy of this girl?"

"No—No," my throttled voice has trembled.

The grip has tightened," "And this girl? Do you know her or not?"

"That...when have I denied that! I do know her. The girl at the balcony of the third flat in the next lane. I have seen her many times, standing in the balcony, her face peering through the blue and violet flowers which fill the balcony. Like a freshly washed Lily...and, passing through that lane, below that balcony, my carefree son! In a tracksuit for jogging in the morning, waving about his tennis racket in the evening, every pore of his body oozing energy and liveliness! He is fond of body building, jokes and laughter – creating a loud and lively atmosphere around him!"

When the girl was doing the trial make–up, even then he used to harass and tease all the girls who had gathered there by his wisecracks. Reduce all of them to helpless tears of laughter.

"I hope you are feeling well now Auntie?"

"Hmm?—Yes—Yes."

"Your blood pressure had become really low during Medha's wedding!"

"Yes..." while saying this, I was wondering how

without any direct reference, this girl was also weaving around the same incidents, the same segments of time, as I was. How she comes and stands nervously, to the same exact spot, around which I too am wandering.

My conscience was prodding me to admit I will never be able to repay you for how much you looked after me when I was suffering from the low blood pressure. But I immediately stopped myself from making this stupid mistake and, keeping aside the talk of gratitude, blurted out another clichéd remark –

"And...how is everybody at your home?"

"They are alright, Auntie."

I was alert and deliberately asking only such inane questions, so that none of them gave her an opening to foolishly cross the boundaries we had created. And that is exactly what happened. She remained reduced to helplessness. The silence spread, and stretched, till it magnified our awkwardness. All through, her lips opened and closed, involuntarily, like the fluttering wings of young birds.

But, now she has controlled her trembling lips and somehow, mustering all her courage, she has asked, almost pleading—"Auntie, any address or whereabouts of the place where you are going?" And, when our eyes meet, a frightened addendum, "Mummy was asking."

"Hmm?...Address?...Where? Well, nothing is known about our future address since it is too early.

A spontaneous and weak response—"Yes, fine. I understand."

Her empty eyes, like a lake shimmering through a dense fog, disappointed, empty, almost begging a question—'Auntie, do you really not understand?'

Not even when, understanding the pain of my empty eyes, a young Jaya had asked me casually, "Auntie, how do you find Snehal?" And she had added on her own, "She is a very good girl, Auntie. Very shy, honest and guileless. Not one to cry about or narrate her sorrows to anyone. My mother often says that if I had a brother, Auntie, then she would have...." Jaya had used all the maturity her young age had given us, to try to look into your eyes and gauge your reaction.

Yes, Jaya had said it, as intensely as her youth and courage permitted. But, perhaps because the signals were clear, I had pretended not to understand the same. Maybe this feigned ignorance was my biggest understanding. Though I could see thousands of images of my carefree, happy-go-lucky son whenever she raised her eyes. The stadium reverberating with tennis shots in the nets of her eyelashes. Her eyelids lift and, with a sharp whistle, my son swimming in free-style in her wet admiring eyes.

Oof! I looked at her, frightened—what if this girl starts crying. But she gives the same vulnerable, sad smile.

I am astounded. Is it possible for anyone to smile like this?

Stop – Stop, at once, right now...this is the climactic moment of all my creativity. Stop—the brightly coloured Roses and the calm Asters! Please stop—emotions, feelings, sensitiveness and all my warm experiences! And also the tears from the eyes of this girl...!

Everybody stop wherever you are! Right now, immediately, first I have to put life in the story I am writing. Are there any more joyous, ecstatic moments for any writer or composer? Oh! What a sad but touching love story! So different from the ordinary, superficial love stories.

"Auntie...."

The ecstasy of climax and putting life into the story is broken.

"I think I should go now...." eyelashes are lowered like petals falling. "Probably we will never see or meet again, isn't it Auntie."

A few words, spoken after gathering all the strength, collecting every ounce of courage. Trembling lips...as if they contain all the turmoil of a midnight's sea storm within themselves.

And that sea has just retreated after banging its head against my stony heights.

"Probably we will never...."

"Of course not. Nothing like that. People keep on meeting and parting in life. Here, would you like a chocolate?"

She had extended her hand in the same refined, cultured manner. And then she had stood up, as if after composing and collecting herself from all sides.

"I will take your leave now Auntie...."

Anguish in every word.

Handing back to me, all that was mine, untouched and as they were.

Light headed with relief and confidence, I suddenly blurt out the most illogical thing –

"Yes, listen.... Why don't you have lunch with me?"

As if it also was my duty to give something in return.

She declines most courteously; her mother would be waiting for her. She had dropped in, just like that, while returning from college.

"Bye... Auntie...."

Oh! This girl, so close to tears, has smiled with the same grace and exited gradually out of the door.

A story has constructed itself, very moving, one of a kind.

In all honesty, I felt like running after her, to cup her forlorn face in my palms and say that, yes, I know why you had come and what you wanted to tell me, and what you are going back without telling me. I know what you want and, probably, I can even give you that. Every flutter of your eyelashes has an image of my son, without him knowing.

But you must forgive me, I want you to understand that I want to keep my son away from your very pure, unblemished, delicate feelings.

And oh – this is the soul of story.

So? I have enacted the pathos of the story in my real life.

The girl walking away, looked back one last time from afar, and was gone.

I return, and while caressing the white Asters kept on the cornice, wonder where the girl would have gone, after departing from here?

Probably to one corner of the terrace of her home, to sit in the shadow of the parapet and write a letter, without an address.

And she will keep searching for an address for that letter, for the remaining years of her life.

Suddenly, I lift my eyes in surprise. The Asters are looking at me with confused and wide eyes.

I have come away, confused.

As if the Asters have seen, not the girl, but I, sitting in the shadows of the parapet, writing a letter without any address.

□

11

Paper Boats and Silver Hair

I am very young. He too was like me. Only that he studied 2 classes above me. I am sitting on the spiral staircase of our mansion and reading very loudly the story of the "Princess with Golden Hair" from the book which has many colourful pictures. He is listening with his chin resting in his palm.

Once, there was a Princess. She was very beautiful. Her hair was Golden. Champa flowers used to fall when she laughed—and when she cried, her tears were a cascade of pearls. One day the Princess was bathing in the river. A strand of her Golden hair snapped. The Princess placed that Golden strand in a bowl made of leaves and let the bowl flow down the river. The cup flowed a very long distance in the river, to where a Prince had come for hunting. When the Prince was tired and thirsty, he came to the river bank. As the Prince was about to drink a handful of water, he saw the Golden hair in the cup flowing in the river. The Prince took the Golden hair strand from the cup and returned with it to his palace – and stubbornly insisted to the king that he wanted the Princess with Golden hair.

"Have you seen a King's palace?" he suddenly asks, removing the hand from his chin.

"No. Never. But father once took me to the mansion of a landlord—he had a very big mansion."

"Bigger than even YOUR mansion? Very big?"

"Yes. Very Big!"

"And kings have palaces that would be many times bigger than the landlord's mansion, no?"

"Then what? Did you think they would be like your five quartered tenements?"

He laughed out loudly. I too laughed. The very idea of a comparison between the lowly Five tenements and the king's palace was so ridiculous that it made us roll about on the floor, laughing out loudly. And all the people working nearby, both labourers and superiors, were staring at us strangely and with distaste.

The Five tenements was a crumbling building, built on a piece of barren land in front of our mansion, which consisted of 5 one-room dwellings with a verandah each. Somebody had constructed these tenements to get some rent from the otherwise infertile land. In one of these tenements, he lived with his parents and younger brothers and sisters.

We studied in the same school. He was senior to me by two standards and I junior by two. I went to school in a Tonga, he walked to school. But even then, we started from home at the same time and returned from school at the same time. This was because, though on foot, he would go by shortcuts through the small lanes and narrow paths, bounding across fields in his long strides to reach earlier—whereas while my Tonga would go by the broad tarred road—the Tonga driver shouting at pedestrians to give way and driving slowly and carefully. He wore chappals and I had sandals with buckles. Often, as I alighted the Tonga upon my return from school, I would see him returning too. He too would be cutting across the fields, jumping up and down while twirling his school bag over his head. We would then talk for long—about what we were taught that day. Which poem I had been taught to sing and which one he had been. We would sing to each other the tunes we had learnt and recite the "Tables" which were taught to us that day. Then he would go on to his Five tenements and I to my Mansion.

I was not permitted to go out of the mansion and he was not allowed to come into the mansion. This was never specifically said or articulated by anyone – it was just one of those things that are understood and accepted. His visits were never banned. He would come, we would jump around near the sun-shade blinds in the veranda or elsewhere in our compound. And read many books with colourful stories. He used to ask with wonder—"Tell me—how big do you think Royal Palaces would be?"

Or then again—

"How beautiful must the Princesses be?" I would retort jealously "Humph. If they have golden or silver hair, they are bound to look beautiful, isn't it?"

Suddenly he burst aloud in a peal of laughter. I asked, "And why this laughter?" He replied "I am thinking if your hair were to become golden, how would you look?"

I was just not able to imagine this sudden fantastic thought about myself. I faltered—"You fool! How can I have golden hair—I am not a Princess."

"OK then, silvery hair at least; shining silvery hair."

Suddenly I remembered, my old aunt had silver hair....

"Oh—if I had silver hair, then I would be old. How can I look beautiful if I am old?"

"Why not? Why would you not look beautiful? You will certainly look good—very good. Much better than you look even now—with hair like silver strands.

He was engrossed in this thought and continued to laugh—without venturing close to the idea of me as an old hag. He was a fun-loving boy and laughed easily....

He was a great mimic too—the scolding of the school teachers, the telling-off by the angry peons, the carping of the Priest who led the prayers. Whenever we got together, he would mimic all of them one by one—and I would go into paroxysms of laughter. It became so that even when he was not around, I would still laugh aloud thinking about his parodies.

Then, the people around us would give us strange and puzzled looks.... Those remembrances still continue, even today when I am a lot older. Any incident in my daily life can trigger the memory of a related episode, and I start smiling for no apparent reason. I am jolted back to reality when my husband or my children prod me and tell me to come back to the present. There is a momentary, unnamed guilt that envelopes me. But since it is now quite rare that I am surrounded by my husband and children, whenever "he" gets a chance, "he" jumps in through the window and we start our endless prattle and teasing—and laughter. Sometimes, serious discussions too—

Like, while eating the tiffin in each other's lunch box, I say—"How soft are the rotis (Indian breads) you get in your lunch box!"

"Yes, my mother applies fresh butter to these. A small amount of sugar also—you also should tell your mother to apply some butter—"

I say "My... I have no mother."

He is confused and I can see his face falling,

"Then who prepares your lunch box?"

"My maid servant."

"Who combs your hair into plaits?"

"My elder Aunt—"

"And who gives you medicines when you are ill?"

"Sometimes father, sometimes maid servant, sometimes Chameli—"

"And who slaps you on your cheeks, when you make a mistake?"

"No one...."

This was a very strange thing for him. He was silent for some time, as if he was noting all this down, and then suddenly blurted—"Don't you get scared at night?"

It was not a small question. It was longer and deeper—what do you do then?

"Well, I start by calling my old Aunt—but you know she is little deaf—then I call Chameli—but she is usually too tired as well. She says in a sleepy voice—Oh, there is nothing my child, go back to sleep, go to sleep my baby.... Or she tells me to recite "Hanuman Chalisaa" and then turns over and goes to sleep herself."

"Then I ask him, "Do you have a mother?"... What is she like?"

He gives a peal of laughter, as always. "My Mother? You will laugh if you see her. She does not wear spotless white sarees like your Aunt but dirty, ordinary sarees and, with a spot of sindoor on her forehead, keeps making hot round rotis on the fire. She does not have any cream or powder, but she makes butter milk, curds, butter, all from a half sair of milk and then uses the same greasy fingers to soften her face and hands before she takes a bath, and she applies a lot of red paint on her feet."

"Will you show me your mother?"

"Yes—Yes, you can come, but how? "

And so, on one of those days, I had suddenly jumped out of window one afternoon and run to the Five tenements, hand in hand.

His mother and sisters were very much surprised and amazed—as if he had done some forbidden but brave deed—as if he had picked up and brought an object, very rare and unattainable....

"This—she is Raaji—daughter of those who live in the mansion—Rajrani—"

His mother kept on looking at me with an enthralled look—as if like a very nice, soft and expensive cloth. "She is the one who eats your rotis smeared with butter and sugar everyday. She does not like the oily parathas, vegetables and pickles given by her maid servant at all. Not even the mohanthal and imaratiyaan." It was not as if he was praising - just telling it as a matter of fact.

His younger brother kept running his hands over the fabric of my silken frock and his sisters kept darting glances at my sandals with buckles.... I was the high point of their day.

Suddenly, he said, "She doesn't have a mother at all" (No sadness or sympathy here either—just a statement of fact).

And lo—it was as if something had jolted and stilled their hitherto glowing faces. All faces went blank—then he spoke, as if to wake them up "but she has a maid servant, she has Chameli, a watchman and an old Aunt at her home. A gramophone with a conical loud-speaker, even tiger skins...even her watchman has a coat and her father has an English hat!..." ...as if he was talking of marvels from another world.

I too saw no fewer marvels in his house. The mesmerising effects of my Silken Frock and Buckled Sandals lasted for a very small period of time. Soon, one of his sisters started paying with me—going round in circles (chakari) while holding both our hands—while the other sister started drawing ikadi—dukadi (hopscotch) squares on the floor in front of the house.

The younger brother and sister then hung on their mother shoulders, pleading for the colorful balloons and flutes to a passing vendor. The brother became so insistent, his mother had to smite him on his back—wham. This made all the other children laugh uproariously and the brother flail his hands on the floor, bawling loudly. The arrival of a wandering minstrel with a dancing monkey made the brother forget his crying and run with all the children to see the "Monkey Dance." Since the younger brother was not able to run as fast as the others, his elder sister carried him in her arms, to keep pace with the others.

When we returned after watching the monkey dance, his mother gave me freshly baked, wonderfully soft rotis, with a little butter, to eat in a bronze plate.

Then, with a lot of affection, she asked me—

"You like these rotis, don't you?"

I nodded my assent, while eating.

"I have taken out the butter just now for you—these kids anyway eat this everyday."

He laughed—"this means that we all will have to eat dry roti and salt tomorrow – isn't it?"

"So what?"

His younger brother said innocently, "If she comes here every day, then will we have to eat dry rotis daily?" Everybody had a hearty laugh at this. Mother said—"who will allow her to come here daily? Now take her back quickly. Otherwise she will get a scolding."

His mother had guessed rightly.

On return, there was the loud roar of father—and a resounding slap with it. Auntie pulled me away quickly and started putting an ointment on the red finger lines which had started appearing on my cheek. While applying the ointment, auntie was trying to make me understand my fault—"My child, please try to understand the prestige and status of your family. Your father's standing is hurt by such actions!... You have no idea how court appearances he has made, how much money he has spent, to finally win custody from your mother.

That day, I was apprised of the fact that I too had a mother.... Too young to fully understand words like "Prestige", "Family Status" and "Our Mansion" ...but trying to understand the meaning of "Insult"—brought about a vision of a small dollop of butter melting on a hot roti in my eyes. That's all....

As a grown up, I understood that since my father had won me in a court battle, which was a symbol of prestige of the family and the strength of his position in the society, he, therefore, somewhere in his mind, wanted that I behave like his daughter—and not like the daughter of my mother. This story of my mother and my father became a part of my life, entangling itself at every small or big corner of my life. I was always linked with the sad fact of being the daughter of separated parents, in spite of all the achievements and the social respect I had. Even after my marriage, at my in-laws house. Even in front of my children—though just as a discussion...without any negativity or any criticism....

After that day, I never went to his house. I was down with a high fever for 8-10 days. Even after my recovery from fever, I was under the observation of my servants, as per the strict instructions given to them for my well-being, health and comfort.... I would wander around in the courtyard, rooms, terrace and balcony of our mansion.

And suddenly I saw one day—a few cots and mattresses, some kitchen utensils, a few domestic items—loaded on a push-cart. The family members were also following the—going to stay somewhere else in the city.

I still stay in the same city. Father has bequeathed all land and property, including the mansion, to his beloved daughter, hard-won in a court battle. My husband and sons look after everything now.

But I still await something improbable. Sometimes, I am jolted by a wave of feeling—whenever I feel that all of them may also be staying somewhere in this city.

Why did it all not end at that age? Why is there still a regret? And for what? Why do I see him sometime, sitting on the stairs, laughing loudly, having effortlessly leapt our years of age—again before I could?...

Whenever I am sad—he effortlessly jumps across the paths and fields, laughing, and vaults in through my window. My sarees turn into pleated frocks – and my feet have sandal with buckles on them....

"Raaji come on. Let's go...."

"Where?"

"On to the mounds of wild berries—or to pluck the red beads from the shrubs behind your mansion—or to make Paan (betel nut) from the leaves of the Peepul tree and to take out thin chironji seeds from the dried pods"

Oh! How does he know that I really do want to make Paan out of the leaves of the Peepul Tree, sprouting in the cracks of old walls; and want to collect red beads and to go through dry wild pods....

"But my husband, children—their breakfast—meals...."

"Why should that stop anyone? After you finish all that or in a break...."

Really?

Just now, standing in front of the mirror, I suddenly notice a line of white hair, starting from right corner of my head. I am lost in an unknown sadness when he laughs loudly behind me – "did I not say that you will look beautiful, very beautiful with hair like wires of silver?"

And I turn back from the mirror, fully assured and confident. As if I am wearing a silver crown on my head.

Outside it is raining very heavily and the wild tree, which stands far away at the centre of playground, is drenched in rain.

I have suddenly turned and started to make colourful paper boats, big and small, out of thick and glossy paper from bright colourful old magazines.

My mature, grown up son is perplexed and asks me—"Mummy...this...what is this?

"Boats...." I laugh aloud with pleasure—"Come, let us put these boats in the fast gushing water at the sides of road—why don't you take few boats as well...."

He is a little stunned and hesitates initially—but then picks up the remaining boats. The boats look like small birds in his fists. And, in the midst of the falling raindrops, just to humour me, he comes along with me and launches the boats, one by one, in the rapid stream of water gushing down the slope.

I am brushing away the water from my head, delighted and enthralled, looking at the boats—moving away, dancing, stopping, again flowing with the strong current of water....

And suddenly, as if in a dream.... I see the rain water flowing in surges, down the slopes and reaching a door of a house. There, a young boy shouts with glee and picks up a boat and looks into it curiously—at a hair, like a silver thread, kept in the boat....

□□□